Alex pulled back from their kiss

and jammed his sunglasses onto his forehead, desperate to look into Taylor's eyes, needing to know she was just as overwhelmed as he. Their kiss had been electric, the arcing passion sizzling between them like an open current.

"Don't stop," she pleaded.

"We must."

With her face tipped up to his, he watched her eyelids flutter open. Her pupils were dilated, her expression needy. He'd never thought she could want him—not with such unfettered abandon. And he'd never seen anyone so beautiful that the vision scorched him. Her cute little nose, her lips swollen from his kiss and the wistful look of regret when he'd pulled back had fired him into a blazing state of urgency that he'd never experienced in all his bachelor years.

"Kiss me, again," Taylor whispered.

He groaned. "If I do, I may not be able to stop."

Dear Harlequin Intrigue Reader,

Deck the halls with romance and suspense as we bring you four new stories that will wrap you up tighter than a present under your Christmas tree!

First we begin with the continuing series by Rita Herron, NIGHTHAWK ISLAND, where medical experiments on an island off the coast of Georgia lead to some dangerous results. Cole Hunter does not know who he is, and the only memories he has are of Megan Wells's dead husband. And why does he have these intimate *Memories of Megan*?

Next, Susan Kearney finishes her trilogy THE CROWN AFFAIR, which features the Zared royalty and the treachery they must confront in order to save their homeland. In book three, a prickly, pretty P.I. must pose as a prince's wife in order to help his majesty uncover a deadly plot. However, will she be able to elude his *Royal Pursuit* of her heart?

In Charlotte Douglas's *The Bride's Rescuer*, a recluse saves a woman who washes up on his lonely island, clothed only in a tattered wedding dress. Cameron Alexander hasn't seen a woman in over six years, and Celia Stevens is definitely a woman, with secrets of her own. But whose secrets are more deadly? And also join Jean Barrett for another tale with the Hawke Family Detective Agency in the Christmastime cross-country journey titled *Official Escort*.

Best wishes to all of our loyal readers for a "breathtaking" holiday season!

Sincerely,

Denise O'Sullivan
Associate Senior Editor
Harlequin Intrigue

ROYAL PURSUIT
SUSAN KEARNEY

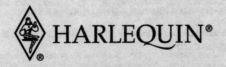

TORONTO • NEW YORK • LONDON
AMSTERDAM • PARIS • SYDNEY • HAMBURG
STOCKHOLM • ATHENS • TOKYO • MILAN • MADRID
PRAGUE • WARSAW • BUDAPEST • AUCKLAND

ISBN 0-373-22690-X

ROYAL PURSUIT

Copyright © 2002 by Hair Express Inc.

All rights reserved. Except for use in any review, the reproduction or utilization of this work in whole or in part in any form by any electronic, mechanical or other means, now known or hereafter invented, including xerography, photocopying and recording, or in any information storage or retrieval system, is forbidden without the written permission of the publisher, Harlequin Enterprises Limited, 225 Duncan Mill Road, Don Mills, Ontario, Canada M3B 3K9.

All characters in this book have no existence outside the imagination of the author and have no relation whatsoever to anyone bearing the same name or names. They are not even distantly inspired by any individual known or unknown to the author, and all incidents are pure invention.

This edition published by arrangement with Harlequin Books S.A.

® and TM are trademarks of the publisher. Trademarks indicated with ® are registered in the United States Patent and Trademark Office, the Canadian Trade Marks Office and in other countries.

Visit us at www.eHarlequin.com

Printed in U.S.A.

ABOUT THE AUTHOR

Susan Kearney used to set herself on fire four times a day. Now she does something really hot—she writes romantic suspense. While she no longer performs her signature fire dive (she's taken up figure skating), she never runs out of ideas for characters and plots. A business graduate from the University of Michigan, Susan writes full-time. She resides in a small town outside Tampa, Florida, with her husband and children and a spoiled Boston terrier. Visit her at http://www.SusanKearney.com.

Books by Susan Kearney

HARLEQUIN INTRIGUE

*The Sutton Babies
†Hide and Seek
**The Crown Affair

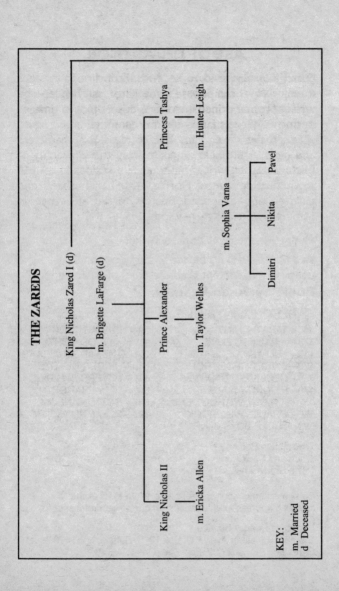

THE ZAREDS

King Nicholas Zared I (d)
m. Brigette LaFarge (d)

King Nicholas II
m. Ericka Allen

Prince Alexander
m. Taylor Welles

Princess Tashya
m. Hunter Leigh

m. Sophia Varna

Dimitri

Nikita

Pavel

KEY:
m. Married
d Deceased

CAST OF CHARACTERS

Prince Alexander Zared—With the help of a stunning American private investigator, can this jet-setting playboy prince uncover a deadly plot in time to save his life, his family and his country?

Taylor Welles—Uncomfortable around men, the pretty P.I. reluctantly agrees to pose as an undercover prince's wife—but she can't remain immune to his charms forever....

Sophia Varna Zared—She's proven to be loyal to her royal stepchildren so far...or has she been waiting for the right time to strike?

Ira Hanuck—Who better to carry out an assassination attempt than the chief of palace security?

General Levsky Vladimir—He has the Vashmiran military in the palm of his hand, but is his allegiance to the crown?

Anton Belosova—The secretary of state's dealings with Vashmiran enemies could be a bid for peace... or war!

For Bing

Prologue

"Highness," Prince Alexander's secretary signaled him through the intercom. "King Nicholas is on line four."

Alex hadn't spoken to his brother in weeks for fear that calls from the royal palace to the Vashmiran embassy in Washington, D.C., might be intercepted. Through diplomatic channels he'd been told to lie low until the person or persons out to assassinate him had been caught.

Anxious over the problems back home, worried about the rest of his family's safety, especially that of his sister Tashya whose life had also been threatened, Alex immediately picked up the phone. "Is everyone okay?"

"Yes," Nicholas reassured him. "General Vladimir's aide and right-hand man is dead, and Tashya is safe." Alex relaxed his fingers, which had been gripping the phone tight enough to crack the casing. Their father had been assassinated last year, and a few weeks ago, Nicholas, the new king, had become a target. And then the general's aide had gone after Alex and their sister. That the traitor was now dead was excellent news. Alex's interminable hiding could come to an end.

As if reading his thoughts Nicholas continued, "My chief of palace security is not convinced the danger is over. We think there may be a conspiracy."

"What kind of conspiracy?"

"We don't know. This may be an internal problem or it might come from one of our neighbors."

Vashmira, a new country founded by Alex's father, had broken away from the former Soviet Union and the new king wanted to strengthen ties to the West. Vashmira bordered Moldova, Turkey, Bulgaria and the Black Sea, and its people were a mixture of religions and ethnic groups. Enemies could come from within or without, and clearly this latest enemy had proved deadly and cagey.

Made restless by his confinement inside the half-finished embassy walls, Alex frowned. "Can you be certain our security chief isn't trying to justify his job?"

"You know better. What you don't know is that Tashya is getting married."

"To the Toad?" Alex couldn't believe she'd knuckled under to Nicholas's pressure for her to marry the crown prince of Moldova when she clearly detested the man. On the surface, Tashya might seem malleable, but she was an expert at getting her own way and neither Nicholas nor Alex had ever quite figured out how she accomplished it.

"I've agreed to a marriage between her and Hunter, the American we spoke about last week."

"Tashya's happy?"

"She's in love. However, the Moldovan government is not pleased. I wouldn't be surprised if they are behind these assassination attempts. It would be prudent for you to maintain a low profile for a few more days."

Weary of remaining in hiding, Alex silently groaned and felt compelled to make the offer, "Maybe I should come home. Attend a few parties…" He often acted the part of the playboy who didn't take politics seriously. It was surprising what kind of information he could pick up at a jet-set party—while enjoying himself. But his new job of ambassador to the U.S. would allow him to help his country in a different way.

"Stay to open our embassy. Right now we need to strengthen our contacts with the West, take advantage of my marriage and Tashya's engagement to Americans."

King Nicholas might speak like a crafty politician, but that didn't mean he wasn't totally in love with his new bride. Alex hoped his sister would be just as content.

He hung up the phone, gratified that Nicholas hadn't demanded that he return. Although Alex had traveled extensively through Europe, Northern Africa and parts of Asia, he hadn't been to the United States before. He'd been eagerly awaiting the time when he could leave the Vashmiran embassy to explore, to accept the dozens of diplomatic invitations he would receive, to meet American women and perhaps to take a romantic sail down the Potomac river. Nicholas may have suggested that he continue to hide, but now that the immediate crisis was over, Alex refused to remain secluded any longer. Long ago he'd accepted that royalty and politicians were always targets and, while cautionary measures at certain times were prudent, he wouldn't spend a lifetime in hiding.

Alex left his office for his private suite inside the embassy and retreated to his living room, savoring the options that would soon be his. He sat at his desk, but didn't really see his papers. He wanted to be free. Free to act like a tourist and to tour the Smithsonian, to enjoy a drink at the Sequoia. Free to explore the Washington Monument, free to taste ice cream from a street vendor, free to enjoy the company of a sensual woman.

Although generalizations could prove dangerous, he often found them to be true. European women had a certain diamond-like sophistication, a je ne sais quoi, a refined style that had been honed for generations and that he'd appreciated with gratitude. In Asia the women were like pearls, each one precious and polished, tending to the men with a respect founded on rituals.

And American women? He couldn't wait to meet them.

Alex savored the idea of just walking down Massachusetts Avenue and Embassy Row. Most people in this country wouldn't recognize him, and for a few hours he could pretend to be an ordinary citizen out for an afternoon stroll. His bodyguards had long ago learned discretion.

Freedom beckoned. His presence here had been kept a secret from all but a trusted few, and if he remained careful, the ever-vigilant American and European paparazzi might not find him for several days. He intended to make the most of his rare opportunity.

Fiery pain suddenly looped his throat.

Alex jerked backward. Raising his hands to his neck, he touched a cruel wire that cut off his air and that was much too thin to grab. He flung his hands away from his neck, frantically searching for a weapon. His fingers closed on the lamp on his desk.

Alex smashed the lamp against the desk and shoved the shards into his attacker. The man screamed.

The garotte around Alex's throat loosened; he gasped in air and shouted for his bodyguards. Behind him, the screams of his assailant ceased, but the unmistakable click of a gun hammer being pulled back gave Alex an instant's warning.

A bullet hissed by his ear as Alex dived through his doorway, rolled to his feet and sprinted down the hall. His suite door was wide open and in the dim light he spied the bodies of his guards, their necks twisted at odd angles. Dead.

Footsteps and the sound of wood splintering next to his head urged him to leap over the bodies and zigzag down the embassy corridor. Cursing under his breath, hoping the blood oozing down his neck was from a superficial wound and that the assassin hadn't nicked an artery, Alex bolted into the grand and uncompleted foyer.

He raced through the nearest exit, past more dead guards. His military training had taught him that the first few moments after an attack could be critical to survival. Without a weapon, returning to fight a deadly opponent would be suicidal. As much as he would have preferred to confront his enemy, he wanted to do so from a position of strength.

Run or hide?

He had just seconds to decide. Pounding down the wide street in the middle of the night, Alex searched for a place to disappear among the dark office buildings and parked vehicles on the block. Seeing nothing promising, he arbitrarily hung a hard right, then a left at the next two intersections.

He told himself things could be worse. He spoke English, was dressed in slacks and a shirt instead of pajamas, and was wearing shoes. His injury didn't appear severe, although it still stung like hell. He had his wits about him, and he'd seemed to have outrun his attacker.

Unfortunately he was lost in a strange country. He knew no one here.

He had no identification and no money. But somehow he would manage, he was sure of it.

And then a car turned the corner, its headlights locking onto him like a heat-seeking missile to a hot target.

Chapter One

Taylor Welles told herself she wasn't destitute. She had enough money in the bank to make next month's payment on her new office building and on the apartment she leased. However, a new client and an influx of cash would be welcome, especially when she added up her credit card bills for her struggling business. So early this morning she'd pretended to be her own secretary, answering her phone in a sweet Southern voice and setting an appointment for ten o'clock with a man who only gave her his first name—Alex—and who undoubtedly believed the private investigator he'd be seeing, Taylor Welles, would turn out to be male.

However, if Alex had been surprised by her gender, he'd covered his thoughts with a nod of his imperious head and a firm handshake. And then he'd sized her up just as carefully as she had him. Dressed in a custom-tailored shirt and slacks that were expensive, albeit a bit rumpled, he settled into the chair opposite her desk like a man on a mission, but he'd carefully hitched the material above his knees to prevent further wrinkles. He seemed to be full of contrasts. His perfectly cut black hair looked as if he'd styled it with his fingers, and he needed a shave. The diamond-studded gold watch on his wrist, the costly Italian leather shoes and an emerald-and-diamond ring allowed her to overlook the smudge of dirt on his slacks, the rip at the shoulder of his shirt and the droplets of dried blood on his collar.

Despite the wild story the man had just told her about an attempted assassination, he looked as if he'd just climbed out of some woman's bed—a woman who had dragged him back for a second or third go-round.

Taylor recognized his type all too well. Her income came primarily from women who suspected their husbands of cheating. And they always were. Sometimes she felt guilty taking her clients' money, but a girl had to make a living, and there was a certain satisfaction in giving her clients evidence they could use against their spouses in divorce court.

She would have enjoyed taking on a different kind of case, but after hearing this potential client's story she wondered if she should call the cops. He sounded as if he'd escaped from the loony bin rather than from an assassination attempt. But he didn't seem threatening, so she would hear him out.

And she had no other work this afternoon. In fact, she had no other work for the rest of this month. Besides, if the man was lying, he was truly good at it. His recollection of details amazed her, but also made her suspicious. People running for their lives didn't usually remember a strange city's layout, and he'd made it all the way from Embassy Row at Dupont Circle and Massachusetts Avenue to her office in Foggy Bottom in a panicked run? Not bloody likely.

One fact led credence to his story. From ear to ear around his neck coiled a raw wound that had recently stopped bleeding but must still be painful. Alex ignored the injury, didn't call attention to it by fiddling with his collar, and that in itself made her curious about him. In her experience most men made a huge deal over every little nick and cut. Her drunk father certainly had. So had her ex-husband. But Alex hadn't so much as insinuated she should help him on account of his laceration. He didn't even seem to want to talk about it, never mind convince her how brave he was.

She needed more details before she could make any decisions. Skilled at subtly extracting information, she didn't allow her doubts to show. ''The car's driver spotted you in the headlights?'' she prodded. ''What did you do next?''

He didn't hesitate. ''I noticed a brown pole topped by the letter M with a red stripe beneath,'' he told her. His English diction was excellent. He claimed that he came from a country called Vashmira and that English was one of their three native languages. Taylor now wished she'd paid more attention to geography, but who could keep track of all those nations that had broken away from the former Soviet Union?

''You took the metro?''

''Who would have thought the subway would be my salvation?'' He grinned, almost self-mockingly.

Obviously a man of his wealth traveled in limos. Good, he'd be able to afford her fee, with a hefty up-front deposit. Maybe she'd even pay off her credit card balance this month—that would be a first.

"The metro cars are air-conditioned and the seats upholstered, the stations well-lit and clean. I was most impressed."

Like she cared? His words didn't sound condescending, but as if he intended to file them away for future use—almost as if he wanted to duplicate the District's metro system. "What are you, a transportation expert?"

"Nothing so specialized I'm afraid."

He still hadn't told her his last name, or what he did for the Vashmiran government, but she let it pass. If she took him on as a client, she would eventually need to know much more than he'd already told her, but she'd learned to temper her curiosity, and not to scare away a customer by asking too many uncomfortable questions before she'd won their trust…and had accepted a hefty deposit.

"I rode the Red line to Judiciary Square where I switched to the Blue line. Now, I'm here. Do you think you can help me?"

She leaned forward, staring into his compelling blue eyes, well aware that he'd left out the hours between the middle of last night and this meeting. "What exactly do you want me to do?"

"Track down the assassins."

Whoa.

She could find somewhere to hide him. Protect him. But track down assassins?

She didn't answer him immediately, but swiveled in her chair to face her computer. After she had entered several commands, her modem hooked into the Internet. She did a quick search of the morning papers, then challenged him. "In a town where last night's rumors are this morning's headlines, there are no stories about dead bodyguards at the Vashmiran embassy."

"Of course not. King Nicholas would demand that the papers suppress the story."

"Things might work that way in Vashmira, but here we have freedom of the press. And how can you predict how your king will react?" She asked the question hoping he would reveal his position at the embassy. He'd spoken so confidently that he either knew the king, knew his country's public policy or was delusional—because he quite obviously believed every word he was saying.

"The king would have asked your government to suppress the news in order to protect me."

"I don't understand," she admitted, and looked to him for an explanation.

"The less information our enemies have, the more difficult it is for them to carry out their plans."

Was he deliberately being vague? She believed so. The man was cagier than he looked. Not for one second would she fall for the charm that radiated from him like seductive cologne. If she bought into his story, which she wasn't sure she did, she had to buy his logic—but he was good at logic, too.

She also noticed that he'd said *our* enemies. Was he talking about his country's enemies in general or about enemies of a particular political party? Until this morning she couldn't be sure that she'd ever heard about the country of Vashmira, and she knew zip, zero, zilch about their political system.

She drummed her fingers on the calendar on top of her desk. A calendar empty of appointments, empty of work. Yet as much as she wanted to take this man's money, she wouldn't lie to him. "Political intrigue is outside my area of expertise. I'm qualified to conceal you from your enemies and to protect you from—"

"That would make a good start."

"—but tracking down assassins?"

"You track down cheating husbands," he countered, revealing that he'd checked up on her, which was probably why he hadn't been surprised to learn that Taylor was a woman. Another indication that he hadn't just shown up on her doorstep by accident. He'd had the forethought to check her out.

Still, he needed to understand that she was not qualified for this particular case. "The difference between searching for a cheating husband and an assassin is like the difference between fishing for trout and shark."

"Look, I need you to tell me where to fish. We can let the authorities reel them in."

He was challenging her to do the work she did best—investigation. She had a nose for finding people who didn't want to be found. She could rarely resist an opportunity to match wits with a husband or wife trying to hide funds during a divorce or with an employee stealing on the job. She'd even taken a few jobs for bail bondsmen. But tracking an assassin?

Sighing, she stalled. "How did you find me?"

"The Yellow Pages." His lips broke into a provocative smile that in no way convinced her that taking this case might be a good idea. And judging by his narrowing eyes, he seemed to know that his smile had failed. "I'll pay triple your going rate."

Triple? She'd only been going to tack on a fifty percent premium for the danger factor. Either the man was a fool with his money—and he didn't look like a fool—or there was something he wasn't telling her.

"Okay. You want to hire me. Here are the terms. I get paid by the day. You cover all expenses."

"Agreed."

"And I need one week's compensation up front. If I solve the case sooner, you'll be reimbursed."

"That could be a problem."

"EXCUSE ME?" Taylor Welles frowned at him. Not a faked, pouty frown with a come-hither gleam in her eyes, but a genuine frown, part wariness, part annoyance, part I-don't-believe-you. He expected her to roll her eyes at the ceiling next, but she didn't seem given to dramatics. She simply stared at him, judging him with calm gray eyes that left him slightly off balance.

With her blond hair pulled straight back from her face in a tense coil, tightly compressed lips with just a hint of lip gloss and high cheekbones that were bare of makeup, she appeared to be all business. Some women pretended to be detached, well aware that men found their distant attitude an invitation to seduction. But he'd been sized up by enough women to recognize immediately that Taylor Welles was different.

And expected payment up-front. "I left the embassy in a hurry. Without my wallet."

"You're broke?"

He shrugged. "Don't you take cases on contingency?"

"Occasionally." She peered at him through narrowed eyes. "How's your credit?"

"In Vashmira, it's excellent."

"We aren't in Vashmira."

He hadn't wanted to use his royal title to convince her to take his case. Maybe it had been pride, a determination to see if he could sway this stubborn American woman by his wits alone. But he'd misjudged her.

So he stood and bowed very formally. "Let me introduce myself. I'm Alexander, Crown Prince of Vashmira."

She shook her head and not so much as one blond wisp of hair came loose. "Okay, I think our time here is over. You can leave now."

He didn't budge, could scarcely believe she intended to throw him out of her office. "Pardon?"

She waved him toward the door. "Go. Vamoose. Scram. Be gone."

He chuckled, a laugh that began low in his stomach and tickled its way up his throat. "You don't believe me?"

"Duh." She picked up her keys and stood, eyeing him as if he were no better than a bum.

"You're making a mistake," he told her, not bothering to contain his amusement and realizing he hadn't had so much fun in weeks.

"It won't be my first mistake. Or the last."

"But why give up such a lucrative commission,"

Alex coaxed, "when you could simply check your computer to see if I am whom I claim to be?" He crossed his arms over his chest, finding that he was enjoying this verbal sparring with Taylor Welles much more than he should have. She was so not interested that he couldn't wait to see her expression when he proved his identity.

"You're wasting my time."

The more she dug in her heels, the worse she would feel when she realized her mistake—which could work in his favor. "Take just one moment more. Punch my name into your search engine. I'm frequently in the tabloids. A picture shouldn't be hard to find."

She threw down her keys. "Fine. But when your face doesn't match—"

"It will."

"—then you'll go?"

He nodded. "And if I am who I claim, you'll agree to take the case?"

"Sure."

"On contingency?"

Her glance went from the cut at his neck to his watch and ring. "Why not pawn the jewelry?"

"The ring belonged to my mother. The watch was a gift from my father. I will never willingly part with them."

He thought her eyes might soften when he mentioned family but the opposite occurred. She stared at him, her eyes gray chips of ice flickering in a stormy sea.

Without another word she sat behind her desk and

this time her fingers flew across the keyboard. She kept looking from him to the images on her monitor, her face hardening with resolve as the realization struck.

"So you are the prince of Vashmira."

"Yes." He'd expected an apology, a change of attitude.

Instead she practically glared at him. "You weren't kidding when you said you were popular in the tabloids."

There was not the slightest hint in her tone that she was impressed with his title or his position. She obviously found the headlines and pictures distasteful, barely glancing at them—or maybe she realized how much of those stories were pure fabrication.

Fascinated by the range of expressions on her face—wariness, suspicion, resignation—he noted just minor irritation as she flicked off the computer—not exactly what he'd been hoping for. But any emotion was a start.

She drummed her fingers on her desk and stared at him. "I suppose you can't phone home for funds since any calls to the palace might be traced back to you."

"Exactly."

"Hiding you is going to be tough. I suggest you lose the ring and the watch right away."

Good. She was taking his case. Although total failure had never entered his mind, he had never expected her to hold out this long. She was tough and apparently a woman of her word.

He hadn't been in the States long, but he understood that she'd mentioned the jewelry because she intended to conceal his identity. Carefully he tucked the ring and watch into his pocket.

"Better." She stood and placed her keys in her purse. "I'll need more information before I can plan my investigation. How about lunch?"

She'd offered the invitation without a hint of coyness in her tone. There was no flirtation. No innuendo. She couldn't have made it clearer that he was simply another client. Perhaps he should have been insulted. But after a lifetime of women flirting with him, he found her attitude refreshing. She expected nothing from him, not smiles, not charm, no grand effort to make her comfortable with his title.

And because she didn't require him to think of these things, he could focus on her while she stared at him, her head cocked at an angle, her lips pursed. "From those tabloids—" she spoke as if *tabloid* was a dirty word "—I'm going to assume that you aren't as popular as Britain's princes and that maybe only half the female population will recognize you."

She'd obviously tried not to reveal her distaste for the party-boy behavior portrayed in the tabloid articles. But her disapproval ran too deep. A slight hitch in her tone had given her away.

He tried to reassure her. "I don't believe my face is well known here."

"We can't take that chance." She opened a closet and tossed him a Redskins cap.

He caught it, adjusted the plastic snaps and placed it on his head. "Better?"

"You have any sunglasses?"

"Sorry. I didn't stop to pick them up while the assassin was shooting at me."

"Not funny." She opened her purse, plucked out a pair with a slight scratch across one lens and handed them to him.

He tried to put them on, but they weren't wide enough. "Perhaps you have another?"

"I'll buy you a pair from a street vendor."

They walked out of her office and into the overcast morning casually, not drawing attention to themselves, but she had checked out the pedestrian and vehicular traffic before heading through the door with a professionalism that he found reassuring.

They hadn't gone a block before she stopped at a street vendor and bought him a pair of sunglasses. He slipped them on, appreciating that the darkness at the top of the lenses would protect his eyes from the bright sunlight while the almost-clear view at the bottom would allow him to read even indoors. He recalled from movies that Americans tended to wear sunglasses because they were considered cool, often indoors and even at night. He turned to her for approval.

She didn't comment on the sunglasses. "Ready for some lunch?"

"My first meal in America outside the embassy."

"I should warn you. We have to stay out of ritzy restaurants where someone is more apt to recognize you. Besides, my budget won't stretch that far."

"What did you have in mind?" he asked, eager to experiment and to see where she would choose to eat, curious to finally walk on American streets. His parents had lived in this country for years before his father returned to Vashmira to lead the revolution. Alex had learned English from his mother as she'd told him stories about America. Now, he could finally see for himself.

"How about a hot dog? We can eat in the park."

"A hot dog. That's a sausage on a bun?"

"Close enough." She stopped on the next corner in front of a wiry man who spoke very little English. The enticing scents wafting to Alex's nose made his stomach rumble.

Without deferring to him, Taylor ordered three hot dogs that smelled heavenly, handed him two, wrapped in paper, and kept one for herself.

"What would you like to drink?" she asked.

"Water?"

"Two waters please." She paid, then scooped green stuff onto her hot dog and sprinkled the meat liberally with onions while he examined two clear containers, one filled with red sauce, another with yellow.

She squirted the yellow sauce on top of her hot dog, which was already slathered with onions. "What are you waiting for? You don't want to eat it naked, do you?"

She couldn't possibly have said what he thought he'd heard. "Excuse me?"

"Don't you want ketchup or mustard? If you don't garnish with onions, you'll be sorry."

He had no idea what she meant. "Why?"

"Because if you don't eat onions, then you'll have to smell them on my breath."

"Oh." She'd just made it clear that she intended to eat her onions and had pointed out the consequences, then left the final decision to him—either eat onions with her, or suffer from her breath. He grinned. He happened to like onions and garlic and this very forthright woman who would eat her lunch the way she wished.

Unconsciously he'd been waiting for her to fix his hot dog. In fact he'd expected her to hand him the one she'd prepared, but America was more a do-it-yourself country than Vashmira. Actually the preparation didn't appear too difficult—after all, the meat came already cooked.

He copied her and was quite pleased with the results. Until he bit into his hot dog and half the relish and onions fell out. A glob of the red sauce plopped onto his shirt. But the multitude of tastes swirling over his tongue more than made up for the mess. Either he was hungrier than he'd thought, or he could become addicted to hot dogs.

He couldn't recall the last time he'd eaten while walking down a street, which only added to the marvelous experience. The French had their cafés, the English their pubs. He supposed the closest thing Vashmira had to this outdoor eating was a bazaar or a country fair.

"These are delicious," he complimented her.

"If you say so."

He'd expected her to be pleased with his compliment, but she wasn't. The woman never quite reacted the way he expected. He told himself it wasn't because he was in a new country, or because he didn't know her well. She didn't care whether she'd pleased him, and he found the idea so astounding that he had to mull it over while he swished down the delicious hot dog with cold water.

Was he so accustomed to people trying to please him that when someone didn't he considered them eccentric? Had his titled world been so skewed that he no longer knew what was normal? He didn't know. But for a man on the run, a man whose life was in danger, he felt remarkably alive and carefree. This American woman who had just bought him lunch had given him something most precious—a new perspective.

Even this part of the city captivated him. He'd never seen brick row houses in a palette of pastels. Lilliputian gardens and mature trees seemed to create an oasis in the urban setting of Foggy Bottom. And almost every other person seemed to be walking quickly as if in a tremendous hurry. He found the frenetic pace both intoxicating and confusing—but not as perplexing as the woman by his side.

When a teenager on a skateboard had rolled close, Taylor had stepped between him and the kid. When a truck backfired, she shoved him around a corner. When he'd reached out to steady her, she'd jerked back, her eyes showing a flicker of fear before she once again cloaked her emotions in a cool gray pool—one that didn't let him see beneath the surface.

Alex realized that she might carry a weapon, she might chase down liars and cheats, but not only didn't she flirt, she didn't like to be touched.

Chapter Two

Taylor needed to hear more about Prince Alexander and his country before she decided what to do with him. From past experience she knew celebrity cases tended to have a broader scope than those of the average client. She'd taken on the cases of an opera diva who had been stalked by a rabid fan and a senator who had been blackmailed by an ex-lover. She'd solved both cases quietly, without the press ever mentioning the names of her clients in the news. While she still took on the occasional job for the senator, mostly low-key investigative work, Taylor had never before worked for royalty and hoped that she wasn't taking on an assignment that was beyond her capabilities.

So before she blew next month's rent, before she got in any deeper, she wanted specifics. In this town, where confidential conversations in restaurants could be overheard by undercover reporters looking for a scoop, she didn't want to risk having anyone eavesdropping on their discussion. So she led Alex into a park and found them a bench shaded by a towering oak.

"Who do you think is trying to kill you?" she asked. She'd found the clue to solving a case could often be learned with her clients.

"I have no idea." In contrast to his almost bored tone, with boyish enthusiasm Alex tossed a piece of his leftover hot dog bun to a squirrel.

"Your father was assassinated last year and now your brother rules the country?"

"Correct."

"You are second in line for the throne?"

"Until Nicholas and Ericka have children. Then I'm off the hook."

Off the hook? "You don't want to be king?"

"Would you want to be president?" he countered, his deep-blue eyes drilling her, reminding her that his laid-back persona hid a sharp intelligence.

She contained a shudder. Having every detail of her life under public scrutiny and having constantly to compromise to get anything done was not her idea of an ideal career. She'd seen too much political infighting and backstabbing to ever want the job of president. One of the things Taylor enjoyed most about having her own business was the freedom it entailed. She took the cases that interested her, worked the hours she chose. Slowly and steadily she'd built a solid reputation in the professional community. She played straight with the local cops, collaborated with a few of the more honest divorce attorneys. Ultimately, she envisioned taking on a partner or two, expanding the firm. The idea of running a country held no appeal for her whatsoever.

She eyed Alex, realizing that the prince and the P.I.

actually had something in common: no interest in ruling their respective countries. However, their backgrounds and lifestyles couldn't have been more different. His had been one of wealth and privilege. Hers had been one of survival in the face of a father who'd abandoned her as a child, an older brother who liked to use his fists on his little sisters, and an ex-husband who'd cheated while she'd worked two jobs to put herself through school.

Although she remained close to her sister Diana, Taylor had tried to put the rest of her past behind her. Her mother had died years ago. Her brother was now serving a ten-year sentence in jail for battering his wife. Taylor tried not to think of him or the hell he'd put her and Diana through. Taylor might be only one month from financial disaster but in the world she came from, that was a luxurious cushion. One she might lose if she didn't protect the prince from the assassin.

She decided to start with the basics. "Why would someone want you dead?"

He shrugged—a shrug that told her absolutely nothing.

"Look, if you don't fill me in, I can't do my job." She sat back and let him mull over her statement. Either he would talk to her or he wouldn't. And while those trust-me-baby-blue eyes of his might speak volumes, they didn't speak a language she wanted to hear.

He stood and threw the squirrel another crumb, tossed the paper into a trash can and returned to the bench. He didn't sit but paced back and forth, his long strides making frequent turns necessary.

He spoke precisely, as though accustomed to people hanging on his every word. Yet he wasn't arrogant, only ultracivilized—his calm a direct contrast to the violent wound on his neck. "We've been having some troubles at home. A year after my father was assassinated, a jealous woman tried to kill our new queen and place her own daughter on the throne. The woman killed herself, but because my brother feared a conspiracy and because our father's murder remains unsolved, your government sent Secret Service agents to protect our king and queen.

"We thought the incidents isolated until a few weeks ago, during my brother's wedding, when someone shot at my sister and me. Nicholas ordered me here and an American agent impersonated me back home. The scheme was complicated, but the man behind the shooting was caught."

"His motive?"

"We believe he intended to kill Tashya and me first, then go after Nicholas when the Secret Service agents, on loan from your government, departed. He was killed before he could be questioned."

"Let me get this straight. In the past year your father was assassinated. Then your new queen, the princess and you have all had your lives threatened?"

"We believed the incidents were unrelated."

"You believed? You weren't sure?"

He gestured to his neck. "We obviously underestimated our enemy."

"You only now think there's a conspiracy?"

He ignored her sarcasm. "All these attacks on my family can't be a coincidence. Yet this attempt on my life may not be connected to those. There *are* other possibilities."

"For instance?"

"We've recently had a crisis on one of our borders. It's possible the motive is political revenge or terrorism. Or maybe one of Vashmira's enemies wants to prevent me from opening our embassy in the U.S. and establishing closer ties to your country."

"Or maybe an enemy of the United States doesn't like the possibility of us having close ties to your country. I'd imagine the Russians wouldn't appreciate an American-Vashmiran air base so close to their borders."

"Now you're beginning to understand the complexity of the problem."

She recalled the tabloid pictures of him with so many different women. "Is it possible some woman's family member is after you for more personal reasons?"

"Perhaps," he admitted, his tone honest, his eyes finding hers and holding her gaze. "But you should know I don't make promises to women I don't keep."

"I'm not here to judge you," she told him, meaning it. She might require information to concentrate on her job, but his lifestyle meant nothing to her. She believed in a live-and-let-live philosophy and had no intention of trying to change the world. She had enough trouble keeping her own neck above water, enough worries about her business and a younger sister who thought she'd just fallen in love. As for Mr.

Lothario, his morals and love life were no concern of hers. Absolutely none.

So what if other women thought him attractive? So what if they flung themselves at him with no regard for their own self-worth. Taylor had made that mistake once, compounded it by marrying the scoundrel, thinking her love would be enough to change his roving ways. Now she knew better.

"You may not be here to judge me, but you don't like me, do you?" He challenged her with a direct look. She found it difficult to continue to meet his gaze but made herself do so.

She didn't appreciate the man-woman undercurrent that he'd suddenly inserted into the conversation. She didn't need this kind of distraction. Perhaps he'd caught a flicker of distaste in her eyes when she'd seen the tabloids, perhaps he'd picked up something in her tone. Her marriage and divorce had not been pleasant and those pictures of the prince cavorting with myriad women had brought up memories she'd rather forget.

Stick to business.

She didn't bother to answer his question and looked from the pavement back up to him. "Tell me about security at the embassy. You think it was an inside job?"

To her relief he didn't insist that she answer, allowing her to steer the conversation back to his problem.

"The guards outside my room were killed, as were the ones at the main entrance."

"How did they die?"

"I didn't stop to examine the bodies."

"I'm sorry. This must be difficult for you, but the details are important. I need to know exactly what happened."

"I'd just received a phone call from Nicholas. I'd been sitting at my desk—"

"You were alone?"

He raised a supercilious eyebrow as if he thought her question impertinent or amusing. "Except for the guards outside my door, I was alone. I was thinking over what my brother had said. The next thing I knew I couldn't breathe. My neck hurt like hell and it took a moment to realize I'd been attacked."

"You didn't get a look at him?"

"It was dark. He grabbed me from behind."

He told her about breaking the lamp, fighting back, his mad dash to the street. He hadn't just been lucky, he'd been resourceful and careful. And he'd known enough to know he'd needed help.

"Are you sure the assassin fired at you?"

"I've served in our military. His gun had a silencer, but I recognize the sound of bullets striking wood. Why?"

"I can't help but wonder why the assassin didn't just shoot you when he had the opportunity. Why use the garotte when a bullet would have sufficed?"

He stopped pacing and frowned, his handsome face revealing that he was deep in thought. Obviously he hadn't considered this angle. His fingers went to his neck, lingered lightly on the raw wound. "What are you saying?"

"A bullet is clean, quick and easy. That the assassin used a garotte tells us that his reason for coming after you might be personal.''

''More distressing to my family.''

That he was close to his brother and sister, she had no doubt. She could read his concern for them in his eyes, hear it in his tone.

''I have a few friends I can query. See if any hit men or mercenaries partial to the garotte have been spotted in the District. But it's unlikely anything useful will turn up.''

She was taking this case. Not because she ultimately hoped to earn a fat commission. Not because she felt sorry for him. Not because of his stunning good looks. His concern for his family got to her on a level she didn't want to acknowledge or examine too closely.

''Now what?'' he asked her.

Standing up from the bench, she waited until a woman walking her French poodle strolled out of earshot. ''You need a disguise, new clothes and a safe place to stay.''

''A disguise and clothes will be appreciated. However, I must return to the embassy.''

''Why?''

''To finish several diplomatic agreements, as well as to oversee the building's completion.''

''Can't you complete your diplomacy over the phone? And hire a contractor for the building?''

They ambled along the Potomac, arguing quietly. She appreciated the logical way he countered her every argument, although ultimately, if she did as he wished, his idea to return to the embassy would make her job harder.

"Our embassy is equipped with encrypted phone systems. I'd be compromising Vashmiran national security to speak openly."

"I cannot protect you if you insist on returning—"

"I need your investigative skills not your protection. Suppose we move into the caretaker's cottage that is behind the embassy but inside the gates?"

We? She knew he didn't mean the royal "we," but Taylor and Alex. He'd obviously thought through his plan, so she'd give him the courtesy of hearing him out before she nixed it. "And then what?"

"Yesterday my secretary sent a memo to an employment agency instructing them to hire a husband-wife team of a general handyman and a gardener. I will apply for the job of handyman and you can be the new gardener."

She restrained a laugh. "You've had a lot of experience fixing plumbing, have you?"

He ignored her sarcasm. "It's the perfect cover."

"Except I don't know a pansy from a peony."

"What's so hard about watering, fertilizing and trimming? At night you can secretly set up security cameras or whatever it is that you do. Obviously our systems are inadequate. As handyman, I'll have access to every department. No one will even know the prince is there," he finished.

She stopped in her tracks, faced him and placed her fisted hands on her hips, not even trying to check her suddenly galloping anger. Had he come to her *because* she was female? Had he had this cozy little plan in the back of his mind all along? "You intend for us to pose as husband and wife?"

"It's only for show. Believe me, I don't ever intend to marry. The idea of even pretending doesn't thrill me much, either."

She didn't give a flying fig if he ever married and realized how self-centered he was. Did he think she'd just jump at his beck and call? She wouldn't play that game. Never again. Fearing that her hands might take on a life of their own and actually slap him, she crossed her arms over her chest. "And won't your personnel recognize their prince?"

"You said you could disguise me."

"From a casual glance—not from people who know you."

"Look, I have a reputation as a fashion plate. A clotheshorse. Dye my hair, dress me in overalls and put a tool belt on my hips, and no one will even notice me. Employers who come from the upper classes rarely notice the faces of the people who serve them. Anyway I know how to go unnoticed. I've been sneaking out of the palace since I was nine. Hiding under the nose of my enemy shouldn't be that difficult and will allow us to investigate." He grinned a grin that should have charmed her but didn't simply because she refused to let it.

His idea had merit. Sure, she could hide him, but for how long? To investigate properly she needed to meet the people with whom he worked, and he'd come up with a plan that would allow her access to the embassy and the people there.

She thought out loud. "We'll need to create a fake identity for you."

"Is that a problem?"

"It costs money." She frowned at him, considering his plan, wishing she didn't think they just might pull it off. "I suppose this cottage has only one bedroom?"

He shrugged, his eyes peeking over the sunglasses at her with glittering amusement. "I wouldn't know. I've never been inside it."

"DO YOU THINK blondes really have more fun?" Alex peered into the hair salon mirror where his black hair and eyebrows had just undergone a major bleach job, transforming his dark hair to sun-streaked surfer blond.

Not about to admit that he looked good, Taylor had considered doing the bleach job herself. But she was no good with hair and feared that a poor job would call attention to Alex. She paid the bill, wondering how long her dwindling cash would last. They still had to buy clothes, his tools, and fake identification for both of them. If she had to pose as the handyman's wife, she couldn't very well use her own name, which would pop up in a database reading that she was a licensed private investigator.

"What's next?" Alex asked her, clearly enjoying his new look. She imagined the man would look sexy even if he were gray or bald, and the last thing she should be doing was noticing.

"We shop at Be-Thrifty."

Ten minutes later she led him inside the thrift shop

and watched him take in the stacks of shoes, the secondhand furniture and the people, some having driven there in a Lexus or Mercedes, combing the racks of used clothing. She'd be willing to bet a year's rent the prince had never been inside a secondhand store.

She headed toward the men's clothing. "What size are you?"

"I don't know."

"What do you mean, you don't know?"

"I've never bought clothes...off the rack." He paused to stare at a faded T-shirt that read So Many Men, So Few With Brains.

She bit back a chuckle. "Well, these clothes are nice and soft and already broken in by their former owners."

He peered at her over his sunglasses, giving her a look that told her he understood she was teasing him. However, nothing seemed to mar his upbeat mood. "I think a shirt with a high collar might be best."

"You don't like T-shirts?"

"It won't hide my neck."

She hated that he'd had to remind her of such a basic fact. But she refused to let him know. Instead she breezed toward the stacks of jeans, pulled out a pair of denim overalls that looked as if they'd fit. She plucked a shirt off the rack, handed him both items and shoved him toward the dressing room. "Go try them on."

With a frown he snagged a pair of men's boxer shorts off a table. She didn't ask. She wasn't going there. She absolutely didn't need to know why he needed boxers.

Several minutes later she tapped her foot, impatiently waiting for him to exit the dressing room. He hadn't been the least bit shy about his change of hair color, and she figured he'd be pleased to wear some clean clothes. "Let's see."

"They don't fit."

From his tone, she'd figured wrong. His former good mood and amusement seemed to have disappeared in the dressing room. "Let me see."

"The pants are too long. The workmanship is shoddy."

"Really?"

"There's a rip in the knee. And two of me could fit in here."

"Get out here already."

He opened the louvered door but didn't step past the threshold with even one bare foot. Yet even partially hidden, she thought the change in his appearance remarkable. The baggy overalls, the old shirt frayed at the collar and the blond hair had made a startling difference.

"They're perfect."

"I look like…"

"A handyman?"

"You're enjoying this, aren't you?"

"It was *your* idea," she reminded him. "Have you changed your mind?"

"One pair of ill-fitting pants is hardly enough to deter me."

She turned away to hide her grin. "You'll also need several more jeans, a few extra shirts and a pair of sneakers."

After the clerk rang up their purchases and offered the bag containing all of them to Alex, he seemed a bit confused—as if he was waiting for someone else to step forward to carry his new clothes. He adjusted quickly enough, taking the bag by the handle and following Taylor to a phone booth where she set up an appointment for his first job interview.

"WE SHOULD HAVE bought an instruction book," Alex complained after they'd secured fake ID from a disreputable-looking kid. In a basement smelling of photographic chemicals, the teenager had made them driver's licenses that looked quite real. He'd warned them that if checked against the Department of Motor Vehicle records, the forgeries wouldn't hold up and then handed them Social Security cards.

Now, as Alex and Taylor stood in front of the employment agency doors, he hesitated. He would have preferred to go into the interview prepared. Taylor had instructed him to use an endearment instead of their new names when he referred to her, as there was less likelihood of a slip-up.

"We don't have time for you to read a book on how to do a job interview." She opened the door, but he didn't budge. "You've memorized your new background, dear?"

"I'm a high school graduate and have been working in Florida building homes for retirees. There's just one problem, darling."

"What?"

"My construction knowledge is limited. That's why we should have bought a repair book."

"Sweetie, just pretend you know what you're doing, okay?"

"Back home, my aide would have prepared notes for me. He would have researched the interviewer's background, so I could connect with him on a level of mutual understanding."

Obviously losing patience with him, Taylor reached through the door, grabbed his elbow and pulled him into the lobby, where a receptionist ignored them as she spoke to someone on the phone.

"Look," Taylor whispered, "if you keep using words of more than two syllables, no one is going to believe you're a handyman."

"I'll try to remember that, honey."

"And don't show them your hands."

He shoved his hands into his pockets. "Why not? You don't like my manicure?"

"You lack calluses. You know, the kind that come from hammering nails?"

Their banter ended when the receptionist hung up the phone. Alex approached the young woman and shot her a warm smile. She noticed, her eyes brightening considerably until she noted Taylor's presence at his side. "Yes?"

Taylor shook her head and muttered under her breath. "You just can't help flirting, can you?" Then she raised her voice a bit louder so the receptionist would hear her. "Sweetie pie, you really need this job so don't blow it, okay?"

Alex ignored her remark. He was just being friendly. "I'm here for an interview about the handyman job at the Vashmiran embassy."

"The one with living quarters for a wife," Taylor added. "We do so hate to be apart, don't we, honey bunch?"

Honey bunch? The receptionist didn't appear to pick up on Taylor's sarcasm and gestured to the waiting area that consisted of several chairs, a cheap formica coffee table and a coffee cart stashed in a corner. "Please, have a seat. We're running a little behind."

Alex helped himself to a copy of *Popular Mechanics* and sat in one of the extremely uncomfortable chairs. He perused the articles in the magazine, finding a variety of fascinating topics that ranged the gamut from automobiles to technology to home improvement. He thumbed to the home improvement section and scanned the articles about furniture restoration, precise measurements, installing a brick walkway, a homeowner's clinic and an expert's advice on repairing concrete.

Beside him, Taylor picked up one magazine after another, flipped through the pictures, then tossed it back onto the low table. She fidgeted, helped herself to a cup of coffee without offering to bring him one and then paced, checking her watch every ten seconds and distracting him from his reading material.

"Will you please sit down," he requested. "How can I read when you're as jumpy as—"

The front door opened and a man walked in. Alex recognized Gil Nevins, the embassy's protocol advisor, immediately. He and Alex spoke several times a day over the phone but had met in person only twice, once on the prince's arrival, and a second time when they'd bumped into one another in the hall. Nevins didn't appear even to look their way. He just headed straight for the front desk, but then he turned and spied Alex. "You look familiar. Do I know you?"

Chapter Three

Vashmira

King Nicholas stood behind his desk in his royal office, much too on edge to sit. Two palace guards stood outside new bulletproof double doors; another pair patrolled the private courtyard; security cameras overlooked the roof, the hallways and even his private balcony. He'd traded privacy for security and reminded himself that he still may not have done enough.

Nicholas told the other occupants of the room his sad news from the United States. "All the guards at our American embassy are dead. Even those who were off duty were killed as they slept."

Twelve young lives snuffed out. Twelve families whose sons would never return. Tomorrow morning Nicholas and his queen would meet the plane that carried the dozen coffins. He would make a speech, declare a national day of mourning and hide tears of sadness and frustration.

"Your brother?" General Levsky Vladimir asked in English, his thick Russian accent harsh. One of

Zared I's most trusted men and one of the original revolutionaries, Vladimir had fought at Nicholas's father's side to establish the new republic of Vashmira. The general was first his father's and now Nicholas's right-hand man, one of the few people who knew that Alex had been in the United States at their embassy.

Nicholas forced himself to speak without revealing the icy fear that had gripped him since he'd received a phone call from a hysterical embassy secretary—fear that he would never see his brother again. "Alex has disappeared."

Ira Hanuck, Chief of Palace Security frowned. "Majesty, what do you mean, he disappeared?"

Of late, Nicholas hadn't been pleased with his security chief and had considered asking Ira to retire. His inability to keep up with the ever-changing, high-tech security business had lately proven a detriment to the royal family. Now Nicholas had begun to question the man's loyalty, as well. As distasteful as he found the notion, he had to consider that someone very close to the royal family was mounting a conspiracy against them. First, there was the assassination of his father, then the failed attack on Alex and Tashya and now the assault on the embassy and his brother's mysterious disappearance.

Hence, the need for the third man in the room. Hunter Leigh was a CIA agent and engaged to marry his sister. He was a man Nicholas trusted absolutely. Hunter had saved the lives of his sister and his half brothers, children of his father's second marriage, at much risk to his own. Since he hadn't been in Vashmira when the troubles started, his loyalty couldn't be questioned.

Nicholas reached the west wall, turned and paced in the other direction. "Investigators believe Alex was attacked in his living room. DNA tests are being done."

"Majesty, there was blood?" Ira asked.

"And slugs in his living room wall," Nicholas informed them. "The good news is that there's no sign of his body. There's been no ransom note." But no reassuring phone call from his brother, either.

"Has Alex been to America before?" Hunter spoke for the first time.

Nicholas shook his head. "He knows no one. He left behind his wallet with money, credit cards and identification." Nicholas forced himself to go on. "The hospitals and morgues in Washington, D.C., have been checked. He's not there. He's not in the embassy."

Nicholas paced, clasping his hands behind his back, a trick his late father had taught him to use when he wanted to appear in complete control of his emotions. He seethed with impatience, wanting nothing more than to fly his private jet to the United States to conduct a search. But since he'd assumed his father's duties and been crowned king of Vashmira, his obligations were to his country first.

Although he couldn't go himself, there was much to be done. "General, I want you to take your best men to guard our embassy. I want a show of strength for both our friends and enemies."

"Yes, Majesty. I was to go soon anyway to speak

with my American counterparts about allowing a U.S. air base in Vashmira.''

"You know my views." As much as Nicholas wanted to maintain friendship with the West and to keep such a strong ally contented, he couldn't afford to antagonize the Arab countries nearby. The balance of power in the Middle East was a difficult and ongoing problem.

''It will not hurt for me to listen to the suggestions coming out of the Pentagon, Majesty,'' the crafty ex-Russian strategist told him.

Nicholas turned to his chief of security next. "Ira, I want you to go, too."

"Yes, Highness," Ira agreed without hesitation. "I handpicked the men who died. I'd like to make the arrangements for their homecoming."

"That's been taken care of. Your job in America is to stay at the side of Anton Belosova."

Ira frowned in confusion. "Our secretary of state?"

"He'll step in as our acting ambassador until we find my brother. Our relationship with the United States is too important to leave to anyone else. I want you to protect him."

"Understood, Majesty."

"Gentlemen, that will be all." The general and security chief departed, but Hunter remained behind as Nicholas had previously requested.

"Majesty." Hunter looked him straight in the eye. "There's a very high probability that one of the three men you are sending to the United States is behind the attempt on Alex's life."

"You don't mince words." Nicholas didn't know

Hunter well, but he implicitly trusted his sister's judgment about him. And Tashya thought he hung the moon. Besides, Hunter came with the very best recommendations from within the highest levels of the U.S. government.

Hunter kept his tone low and even. "Lives are at stake. By sending the general, the security chief and the secretary of state to America, you might be signing your brother's death warrant."

Nicholas's stomach churned. He loved his brother, but he had a responsibility to his country and its people. Someone was trying to take over Vashmira, planning one assassination plot, then another. In addition to the possibility of a traitor attempting a military coup or a revolution that would tear his country apart, he had to weigh the lives of his wife, his sister and his three half brothers against Alex's. "If I allow those men to stay hidden in Vashmira, we may never discover who the traitor is."

"You have a plan, Your Majesty?"

"In private, please call me Nicholas. We will be family soon."

"Yes, sir."

Nicholas hated to ask Hunter to leave his sister and go to the United States when they hadn't even had a chance to officially announce their engagement. But he would. The American possessed law enforcement contacts and was well equipped to head an investigation into Alex's disappearance. Besides, if Alex had survived, and if another attempt was made on his life, Nicholas couldn't think of a better man to help his brother.

"I'd like you go to Washington, too."

"To find Alex?"

"To help keep him safe and to ferret out the traitor."

Hunter didn't hesitate. He picked up two pieces of paper and a hole punch from Nicholas's desk. He placed one sheet directly on top of the other, folded the paper then punched random holes. "Since we don't know if the palace phones and mail are secure, I'll send you a fax." He unfolded the two sheets of paper and handed one to Nicholas. "Majesty, you need merely place this paper over my fax to read my message."

"Clever."

"It is extremely difficult to break the random code without the key."

Nicholas folded his paper and placed it in his wallet. "I won't lose it."

"There's one more thing we should discuss. Your sister isn't going to be pleased that I'm leaving."

"She'll understand better than you think. Tashya may appear to be self-centered at times, but her loyalty to her family always comes first."

"I know that. I'm just afraid she'll demand to come with me, and I'd prefer she stay where she will be safest."

"She's lobbying hard for women's rights in our cabinet. With the votes coming up soon, she won't want to leave." Nicholas took a deep breath and let the air out slowly. Although it did nothing to stop the acid burn in his gut, his pulse almost stopped racing. "However, after construction is finished, I'm taking

the entire family to Washington to open the embassy.
I hope you'll have everything under control by then.''

"I'll do my best, but…''

"But what?''

It wasn't like Hunter not to speak his mind.

"If we don't root out the traitor first, placing your
entire family together would be ill advised. You'll be
giving your enemy an irresistible target.''

Washington, D.C.

WARY, TAYLOR EYED the well-dressed man who was
staring at Alex with an I-know-you-but-I-can't-
remember-from-where look on his face. Taylor assumed the stranger had to be from the Vashmiran embassy. Did he recognize his prince, who had taken off
his cap when he'd stepped indoors?

This would be a good test of Alex's disguise. While
she didn't believe the embassy's advisor on protocol
was dangerous, she didn't know he wasn't, either. So
very casually, she placed her hand in her pocket and
gripped her gun. The continuing puzzled expression
on the stranger's face gave her hope that Alex's sunglasses, overalls and new hair color were effectively
disguising his identity.

"I am a handyman,'' Alex told his fellow country-
man. "Perhaps I have fixed your plumbing?''

"Mr. Nevins,'' the secretary said, greeting the man
with triple the enthusiasm she'd given to Taylor and
Alex. "What can we do for you today?''

"I need a private word with Ms. Wilson.''

The secretary pointed to a door. "Just go right through there."

After the door shut behind him, Alex spoke in a whisper and gave Taylor one of his approving looks over the rim of his sunglasses. "My protocol advisor didn't recognize me. I believe this pretense may work."

They didn't wait long before Mr. Nevins exited Ms. Wilson's office and departed without a glance their way. His business over, he didn't appear curious about Alexander, and Taylor relaxed her grip on her weapon.

"You may go in to see Ms. Wilson now," the secretary told them.

After introducing and seating themselves in Ms. Wilson's office, Taylor realized that she didn't have any more experience in this kind of job interview than Alex. Sure, she'd worked through school, but the kinds of work she'd taken at fast-food places hadn't required a sit-down interview with anyone from an agency.

Taylor was beginning to be afraid that their forged identities would not stand up to the kind of thorough background check Ms. Wilson would probably do. But there was nothing to be done now, except bluff their way through.

Ms. Wilson had a round face and kindly blue eyes and could have played the part of the grandmother next door, the kind who baked cookies from scratch and kept a dotty cat. She didn't seem the least bit suspicious about the false work histories Taylor had given her. The forger had provided them with former employment records with businesses that had since gone under or filed for bankruptcy, making reference checks difficult.

"How long have you two been married?" Ms. Wilson asked.

"One year," Alex said.

"Two," Taylor replied at the exact same time, then turned and glared at him. This was her country. He should let her answer the questions. As usual, he responded to her annoyance with amusement, which made her want to get back at him.

When Ms. Wilson chuckled, Taylor turned away from Alex and added, "I'm counting from the time we eloped, not the official wedding ceremony that we had for *his* relatives."

"You both understand that you will be required to live in the cottage and that visitors aren't allowed."

"That won't be a problem," Taylor ad-libbed before Alex could say more, sounding much braver than she actually felt about their new pretend marriage. "In fact, it'll solve my father-in-law problems."

Alex scowled at her. "My father is only trying to help you with our finances."

Taylor smiled warmly at Ms. Wilson. "I assure you that we will welcome the privacy. Since we won't have to shell out a good portion of our salary for rent, we can put a little money into our savings account."

"Well, you both seem eminently qualified." Ms. Wilson stood, walked to her copy machine and made duplicates of the false résumés for her files. "Can you start today?"

"Today?" Taylor hadn't planned on moving this

afternoon, and it seemed a bit too soon to prepare herself to play the role of his wife.

Alex stood. "Of course we can. Is there a reason for the rush?"

"Apparently there are some shoddy construction areas that need immediate repairs." She frowned. "Holes in the walls were mentioned."

Ms. Wilson might not be aware that those holes were due to bullets that had missed their target, or she wouldn't have such a pleasant smile on her face. Or perhaps she was simply pleased to fill the vacancy and thinking about her commission.

Ms. Wilson also stood and shook hands with both of them. "It's been a pleasure doing business with you. The guards at the gate will have your names on their list and will give you proper embassy identification. I hope you'll find the new jobs to your liking."

"I'm sure we will. Thank you," Alex told her.

"On the way out, please stop at my secretary's desk and fill out a few forms."

A few minutes later they left the employment office. The muggy late-afternoon air was heavy with the promise of rain. Dark storm clouds scudded overhead and people hurried on the sidewalks as if sensing that the skies were about to pour down on them.

Alex placed his Redskins cap back on his head. His stiff movements and lack of expression indicated his displeasure. She'd have thought he would be happy to have gotten the job.

"What's wrong?"

"That woman didn't do so much as a cursory check of our credentials."

Taylor thought the interview had gone amazingly well. "That's good for us. We landed the jobs, didn't we?"

"Yes, but do you realize how easily we infiltrated the embassy? We could be criminals. Terrorists. Suppose we were the enemy?"

"How many people have you hired?"

Alex threw his hands up into the air. "Cleaning crews. Construction people. Cooks. Telephone installers. Decorators. Carpet layers. The list is endless."

For the first time since he'd mentioned the cottage, she was glad they would have a place separate from the others. A place where she could secretly install tight security and warning systems. "Once we're inside the embassy, I can sweep the phones and rooms for bugs. Our primary concern should be to investigate people with a motive to want you dead."

TAYLOR HADN'T EXPECTED the cottage to be a two-story Victorian that reminded her of an elaborate dollhouse. She and Alex had returned to her office, picked up her car and driven to the embassy after stopping by her apartment to pack a suitcase and running a few more errands that included buying a tool belt and tools to complete Alex's disguise. He'd handed their employment papers to a guard inside the embassy gate, and in return they had received a key to the front door of the cottage. The guard had issued directions to drive around the modern office building currently

under construction, with instructions to watch out for
the barricades.

"This is a cottage?" Taylor asked, unable to keep
the awe from her tone.

"It's a leftover from the original estate," Alex told
her as she parked her car. "Apparently, a wealthy
doctor built the house for his aging mother. We plan
to tear it down to build a parking garage."

What a shame.

The elegant house had a steep pitched roof, bay
and dormer windows, a single front door and a half
basement with railings around it. They climbed a narrow set of stairs to the front door. So far, from a
security point of view, Taylor liked what she'd seen.
The chimney was too narrow to gain entry from the
roof and she envisioned mounting cameras on the upper shutters where they wouldn't be noticed.

But what made her even happier was the house's
size. To her, a cottage was a one-bedroom cabin with
a combination living-kitchen eating area. However,
this "cottage" obviously had several bedrooms and
that thought eased the tightness in her chest.

Although Alex hadn't done or said one thing that
made her uneasy being around him—he hadn't had
to. His maleness alone made her wary. She thought
she had overcome her prejudice, knew in her head
that all men weren't like her brother, who'd taken out
his anger on his little sisters with punches and slaps.
Most men didn't beat women. She also knew that all
men weren't cheaters like her ex-husband—but
thanks to the actions of the men in her life, she expected the worst and always kept up her guard.

Her sister Diana had told Taylor that her attitude was unhealthy, but that didn't change the fact that trusting anyone with a Y chromosome had become inconceivable. At least she didn't have to worry about trusting Alex; he could obviously have any woman he wanted. He wouldn't be interested in her—a woman who didn't even like to be touched.

Alex unlocked the door and stepped back. She was about to step across the threshold but he raised his hand in a gesture that suggested she halt.

"Is something wrong?"

"We have a custom in Vashmira, when a husband and wife enter their new home for the first time, they kiss for luck." His voice was low, husky, and set her alarm bells jangling.

He wasn't going to kiss her. "We aren't in Vashmira."

"This embassy is Vashmiran territory."

He wasn't going to kiss her. "You're supposed to be an American."

He leaned toward her. "You have a similar custom, yes? When a bride and a groom—"

She wasn't going to let him kiss her. "We aren't married," she told him, refusing to retreat, but somehow she'd backed her rear against the door.

"We are pretending to be married. Married people kiss."

"I believe the operative word is *pretending*."

He crossed his arms over his chest. "Just who is going to believe we are married if every time I touch you, you jump?"

"So then don't touch me." She forced her feet to

advance and brushed past him without looking back. Her pulse was racing just from their conversation, and her scalp had prickled with sweat. Fear had flooded through her with a sickening swell. She hated this weakness in herself, hated that the mere suggestion of a kiss could make her tremble, as though she hadn't learned to put her past behind her.

Alex flicked on the light, but she didn't turn around to face him, didn't want to see his emotions when she was having enough trouble dealing with her own. She distracted herself with the front hall, which had a wooden floor, a charming fireplace, built-in niches and an archway that led to a drawing room. The cottage came fully furnished and there were racks for coats, canes and umbrellas, several straight-backed chairs and a heavily carved chest with a mirror hanging over it. Expensive antiques, she was sure.

She caught a glimpse of Alex in the mirror. He watched her. Keeping his distance, he'd hooked his hands into his overalls as if to keep them from reaching out to her, knowing she needed the room between them to feel safe.

"Did you hear that?" she asked, looking up the stairs where she thought she'd heard a thump.

He shook his head.

Perhaps it had just been the roaring of the blood in her head. Yet her hand automatically reached for her gun. She intended to check the house thoroughly for intruders.

She inspected the downstairs rooms—the drawing room, dining room, kitchen and the study with its dusty billiard table and antique penny slot machine.

Although she heard no additional suspicious noises, she opened every closet door and checked the back door and all the window locks.

"Satisfied?" Alex asked her, his patience obviously wearing thin.

"I need to search the second floor."

"How about I bring our things in from the car?"

He hadn't been out of her sight all day, except to use the bathroom. At her apartment he hadn't seemed the least bit curious; she'd been grateful when he'd waited on the sofa while she'd gathered her things together. Luckily, with most of her equipment in her car trunk from a previous job, she had everything she needed to place a security system in the house.

"I'd rather you stayed with me." The moment the words came out, she realized that she'd implied something she hadn't meant. She thought a playboy like Prince Alexander might make a joke or tease her, so when he simply frowned, she felt relieved.

"Why do you want me to stay inside?" he asked.

"So I can protect you."

She realized the contradictions in her were somewhat ludicrous. She was a woman whose heart raced at the mention of a kiss. Yet she was quite capable of making security arrangements and of protecting the prince with her gun. An expert shot, she practiced shooting and self-defense often. While no martial arts expert, she could deflect a kick or a punch. Mostly she did her job by using her brains and avoiding trouble before it began.

To his credit, Alex didn't point out that he was twice her size and strength. He merely followed her up the stairs. She flicked on the lights and checked out the three smaller rooms, including the closets and under the beds, before heading to the master bedroom.

She flicked on the light. In the second between darkness and light, she spotted a silhouette. A man sat on a queen-size bed, regarding her with sharp eyes that hinted at a keen intelligence.

He ignored the gun she pointed directly at his heart. "Please, come in."

Chapter Four

"Allow me to introduce myself. I'm CIA Agent Hunter Leigh."

His name meant nothing to Taylor, and she kept her gun aimed at the dark-haired stranger's heart. Although he'd been careful not to make one threatening move, she suspected he could. The average thug had neither his kind of clearly superior physical control, which allowed him to remain motionless, nor the will-power to project confidence and radiate charm at the same time.

She had to determine whether the stranger was friend or foe, and really a CIA agent. She wouldn't be rushed, and signaling Alex to remain hidden, she assessed the threat, instantly recognizing that she faced a very dangerous man. While, at the moment, Hunter Leigh didn't appear hostile, his mere presence inside the cottage bedroom warned her to remain on guard.

First, he'd been waiting for them—expecting them—which meant he'd either followed them with-out her having noticed or he'd been thinking several moves ahead. Either option revealed a man with superior capabilities and someone who might or might not know that the prince was about to walk into this room.

Second, Hunter hadn't turned on the lights, which meant he had wanted to keep his presence here secret. And when she had turned on the lights, she'd noted that he had positioned himself so curious onlookers or casual observers couldn't have spotted him through the window.

Third, he wasn't their enemy, or he would never have given up the advantage of surprise and he'd have attacked long before now.

Hunter Leigh meant Alex no immediate harm.

The conclusion brought relief, more than she'd expected. In the short time she'd known Alex she'd come to like him. And if she were ever again to let herself be interested in a man, it would be someone like Alex, someone likable, who didn't take himself too seriously. However, she had no business letting her focus stray from the stranger on the bed.

After considering the circumstances and weighing her options, Taylor replaced her weapon in her pocket. Apparently her action signaled Alex to step around her and to stare hard at Hunter. "I recognize his name."

"But not the man?" Taylor asked, curious at Alex's tone, which seemed an odd combination of warmth and prudence with a touch of judgmental circumspection thrown in for good measure.

Alex confronted Hunter Leigh with the confidence so inherent in his character. "If he is who he says he is—"

"I am." Hunter still didn't move one muscle other than those required to speak.

Puzzled, without taking her gaze off Hunter, she asked Alex, "Just how do you know—"

"Hunter Leigh is Princess Tashya's fiancé," Alex explained, his voice giving no hint of either his approval or disapproval of the betrothal.

Since Alex didn't recognize Hunter Leigh on sight, trusting the stranger could prove to be a huge mistake. For all they knew, he could be the assassin claiming to be Hunter—except if that were the case, he would have been shooting bullets at them, not merely talking.

All the same, Taylor was glad Alex hadn't broken the cover they'd just established for him by admitting that Tashya was his sister. Once again she realized Alex hid a keen mind behind his playboy reputation. He adapted to emergencies, coping well with the unexpected and thinking quickly on his feet. Admirable traits that had kept him alive and had made her realize that first impressions could be oh, so deceptive.

She kept one hand in her pocket close to her weapon and placed the other on Alex's wrist, communicating her distrust of Hunter with a slight warning squeeze. "Can you give us proof of your identity?"

Hunter's eyes locked on Alex. "Tashya said to tell you that she'd prefer to marry me than the Toad."

Beside her, Alex chuckled, his tone warm, light and as rich as chocolate drizzled over fudge cake. He removed his ball cap and sunglasses and tossed them onto the bed.

"The Toad?" she asked, still confused.

"Tashya's pet name for the crown prince of Moldova," Alex explained. "It's an inside joke that she would only tell to someone she trusted."

Taylor supposed she would have to take the intimate reference as proof. Identification could easily be faked, backgrounds manufactured. She found herself trusting Alex's evaluation of Hunter and felt safe with her decision. The prince was no fool. He'd proven that by escaping an assassination attempt, by hiring her, and by inserting them back into the embassy. If Alex believed Hunter Leigh was his future brother-in-law, she could accept his assessment—especially since the prince was fully aware that his life could depend on it.

Hunter stood. Alex walked forward and the two men shook hands. "Nicholas sent you? My sister couldn't have been pleased."

Taylor noted the way Alex's voice softened when he spoke about his family. Without his telling her so, she understood that the siblings were close and that he cared about them a great deal. The first words out of Alex's mouth hadn't been about his current problems and the attempt on his life, but about his sister. Taylor's opinion of the prince rose yet another notch.

Hunter gestured for them to take seats. "Tashya and Nicholas were worried about you."

"Were?" Taylor frowned, remaining on her feet.

"The moment I recognized the prince on the security cameras, I faxed Nicholas that his brother is alive and back at the embassy."

Alex sighed. "You recognized me that easily?"

"I'm a trained observer. Your disguise should be sufficient to fool most people. The blond hair is a clever touch. And the overalls are perfect."

While Hunter's approval of Alex's disguise reassured her, Taylor couldn't help from voicing the nagging worry that had zipped through her. Sending a message to Alex's family could have alerted Alex's enemies to their presence here. She didn't bother keeping the concern from her tone. "Well, I hope you sent that message in code or—"

"I did," Hunter assured her, and then reached into his front pocket. He took out two pieces of paper with randomly punched holes and handed one to Alex. "Your brother and I have matching keys. I made another so you can have one, too. Just place this paper over a coded note and the letters that show through will reveal the message."

He went on to explain that fax numbers were written on the top of the page in case they needed to contact Nicholas or himself. At Hunter's explanation, Taylor felt a measure of relief. Hunter knew his business, and she was glad he was on their side. On the other hand, if Nicholas believed that Alex needed a man of Hunter's obvious expertise, he was confirming her conviction that the royal family had serious enemies. Deadly serious.

Alex carefully folded the paper and stuffed it into the pocket of his overalls. "Does Nicholas know who was behind the deaths of our guards?"

Again, the prince impressed her. He hadn't asked who was out to kill him, but who had shot his guards. Taylor couldn't help respecting such genuinely unselfish behavior—especially in the face of continuing danger.

Hunter shook his head. "While you remain here and keep watch on your fellow countrymen, I'll check my resources for terrorists, signs of political activists and outside threats to Vashmira. However, Nicholas and I both suspect the danger is coming from inside your country. Specifically from someone you trust."

"Who are the suspects?" Taylor asked.

"Three men top the list and Nicholas is sending them all here. Anton Belosova, Secretary of State, General Levsky Vladimir, head of Vashmira's military, and Ira Hanuck, Chief of Palace Security. They arrive tomorrow."

"Their possible motives?" Taylor asked.

"Power." Alex answered succinctly. "Someone is trying to kill off my family and usurp the throne." He slammed his fist into his palm. "The bastards killed my father and now they are after the rest of us."

Taylor looked from Alex to Hunter. "You believe this is a conspiracy? Then why isn't Nicholas being attacked?"

"He was," Hunter told her, "until the U.S. government sent Secret Service agents to protect him and his queen. Right now, Alex is the target."

"Because he's alone and vulnerable?" Taylor asked.

Alex turned thoughtful. "If we play our cards right, we can use their interest in me to our advantage."

Whoa. She didn't like the hard edge in Alex's tone or the responding gleam of approval in Hunter's eyes.

She hadn't been born yesterday. She knew what they intended. They wanted to use Alex as bait.

ALEX TOOK ONE LOOK into Taylor's expressive eyes and was slightly taken aback by the fierce gleam of anger that seemed to come from out of nowhere. She hadn't exhibited one sign of feminine interest in him, hadn't appeared to make even one decision based on emotion, but, instead, had always seemed to use what Alex thought of as sensible logic. While he could never forget that a woman with her terrific good looks *was* a woman, he had been thinking of her as a partner, a competent partner he could count on. Since he didn't have a clue as to the reason for her anger, he assumed she thought Hunter was usurping her position, especially when she glared at him.

Taylor didn't raise her voice to Hunter, but her anger rang through her every word. "I'm not letting you stake Alex out for bait while the stalkers circle 'round and we wait to see which jackal pounces first."

Damn. He'd read Taylor dead wrong. She wasn't thinking about the possibility of Hunter usurping her position. She was worried about him. The realization rocked him back on his heels and created a warm glow. He'd simply expected her to take a back seat to Hunter, but instead she was challenging the CIA man.

Taylor's anger reminded him of another woman. His sister would react in exactly the same way—with loyalty, standing up to any man who threatened her brothers, be they the press, kidnappers or gossips.

Alex suspected that if his sister and Taylor met,

they would soon become good friends, recognizing one another's strengths. Much as he had immediately trusted Hunter because Tashya did, his sister would approve of Taylor.

Alex suppressed his first impulse to soothe Taylor. Instead he took an acute interest in watching Hunter attempt to change her mind.

A man with obvious confidence in his abilities, Hunter looked Taylor straight in the eye. "I won't use Alex for bait—unless he's our last option. You need to understand that King Nicholas has sent over three powerful men—any one of whom could be the traitor. He's giving us an opportunity to flush out—"

"Not at the expense of Alex's life, he's not," Taylor argued.

Interesting. The woman was not just fierce, she could restrain her temper, too. The combination of a hot core wrapped in cool logic struck a chord in Alex. He adored women, liked the variations of femininity, appreciated the differences between the sexes, but Taylor kindled a fascination he had not felt before. She didn't seem to care whether she offended Hunter even though he represented the interests of two countries. She didn't care whether she offended his brother, the king of Vashmira, by messing up his plans. She didn't care whether she offended Alex by speaking as if he didn't have a mind of his own. After all, if anyone decided to risk his life—it would be him. Normally, he would have pointed out this fact, but the temptation to let Hunter argue with her proved too strong. Alex wondered if she'd react this way over any client's life and couldn't wait to hear what she would say next.

"We're getting way ahead of ourselves," Hunter told them. "Right now, we need information. I'm assuming you were hired as a gardener and a handyman to snoop around?"

"You're avoiding the issue," Taylor challenged.

Alex almost chuckled at her persistence. He found her stubbornness in defending him quite charming—especially since she didn't appear to like him. However, he hadn't overlooked the fact that although she didn't like to be touched, she'd voluntarily taken his hand and gently squeezed it earlier. Of course the situation then had been far from amorous, but her action revealed to him where she placed her priorities. He imagined that changing those priorities might prove quite a challenge—one he looked forward to.

Although he'd seemingly made up his mind to pursue her on the spur of the moment; in reality, he'd been attracted to her from the instant they'd met. His interest had only heightened as he'd learned she wasn't feigning her disinterest, but that she flat-out was not interested in him as a man. After watching her stand up to Hunter, the challenge of winning her trust seemed even more difficult and delicious.

Hunter didn't deny that he'd sidestepped the issue of using Alex for bait. "Let's hope that our snooping efforts will reveal the traitor." He offered his hand to Taylor.

She hesitated, then shook it. Hunter nodded to Alex, their gazes locking above her head. Alex nodded slightly, indicating his willingness to do whatever must be done. Hunter took the silent message with him and left, his shadow merging into the darkness of the evening.

Taylor strolled to the window and stared down into the courtyard below. A silence yawned between them that Alex hesitated to break. He didn't understand Taylor, who was different from the other women he had known.

So he hadn't a clue what was going through her head. His instinct was to come up behind her and to put his arms around her. To show her with an action that he cared—since he couldn't find the words. But Taylor wouldn't appreciate such a gesture.

Alex could be patient when necessary. He waited for her to turn from the window. Waited for her to begin a conversation. But she said nothing. Didn't move. He didn't know when it got to be a contest in his head, but he figured that the first person to move or to speak would lose.

He lost.

He joined her at the window. Looked out into the night and saw what she saw. Although the cottage was located at the rear of the embassy, from this second-story window they had a clear view of the front gate. A limousine had arrived. Men unloaded baggage. Three men, one in uniform and two in dark suits, exited the vehicle.

Although their faces weren't clear, Alex recognized them. "The man in uniform with the gold braid on his shoulder and the imposing stature is General Levsky Vladimir. The shorter man is Ira Hanuck, Chief of Palace Security, and the portly fellow in the ill-fitting suit is Anton Belosova, Secretary of State. And if I can see them from here, they can see us. Possibly recognize us.''

''There's always been that possibility.''

He turned to her but she continued staring out the window. ''To pull off this deception, we need to pretend to be husband and wife. Are you up to it?''

Finally she turned to him, amused. ''I'm good at pretending.''

''Really? You jump every time I touch you.''

''Then don't touch me.'' She squared her shoulders and raised her chin as if girding herself for battle. ''Just stand there while I kiss you.''

She couldn't have surprised him more if she'd suddenly decided to leap out the window. She wasn't playing a game. She wasn't flirting. She was very, very serious, confusing him totally. ''What are you saying?''

''Tip your head down,'' she instructed. ''But don't move.''

She intended to kiss him. This woman who had defended him against one of the top agents of the CIA, this woman who wasn't afraid to hunt assassins but who didn't like his touch, intended to kiss him.

Alex had kissed many women. Some of them may even have told them they intended to kiss him, but no one had stunned him as Taylor just had by her simple declaration. Impressed by her determination, if not a little set back by her clear lack of enthusiasm, his blood nevertheless zinged in anticipation.

She lifted her lips to his. ''Don't lean forward.''

''Okay.'' He hid his amusement along with his eagerness. When he stared into her eyes, something about her reluctance tugged at him and he suddenly had the urge to punch out the man who had done this to her.

"Don't raise your arms."

He swallowed hard, not only surprised by his willingness to cater to her every whim, but enticed by the combination of emotions he read on her face: tenacity, conviction and perhaps just a touch of curiosity. She was close enough for him to take in the scent of her hair, a light aroma that reminded him of a fresh spring rain. Without thinking, he started to raise his hand to run his fingers through her hair.

"Keep your hands where they are."

Her soft instructions, whispered in a husky tone, made him ache for her. He found himself yearning for her touch and her kiss like an innocent kid. He'd had women who had taken control, even demanded control, women who liked to dominate, but that wasn't Taylor's way. He sensed that she'd been dominated in her past and the experience hadn't been pleasant. If he could hold completely still, she would feel safe. He could give her safe, for now, but found himself yearning to give her so much more.

Slowly she brought her lips up, her eyes wide open, her pupils not the least bit dilated, her breath steady. He suspected that, while he was as eager for her kiss as a fired-up stallion, she felt nothing but resolve. On the rare occasions when a woman didn't want him, he'd simply headed in another direction. However, this time, he held absolutely still.

Waiting.

Waiting for her to come to him. Letting her feel free, liberated and autonomous. Subduing his every natural impulse had him feeling as if he perched precariously on a high wire, where one sudden move would spoil the fragile balance of the moment.

Could that be his stomach lurching in anticipation of a kiss? Could that be his heart kicking into fourth gear?

"Perhaps..." she whispered uncertainly.

"Perhaps, what?"

"Could you close your eyes? Please."

He bit back a groan. It wasn't enough he'd promised not to move. She didn't want him to watch her, either. Taylor Welles had no idea how difficult just standing there, waiting, could be. She couldn't know that his heart had pumped too much blood to his head, making him light-headed. He was particularly grateful for the loose overalls that kept his swelling erection from her view.

He couldn't recall the last time he'd wanted a woman so badly. But he resigned himself to a long, cold shower tonight. If he got lucky, she might kiss him—but she wouldn't do more. She needed a safety net, so she would never know how ready he was to make love. He could barely believe she had him so aroused with just the promise of a kiss, a kiss he would never receive if he didn't comply with her request. He closed his eyes.

And waited.

TAYLOR DIDN'T KNOW if she could carry through with her bold suggestion. The words and directions had simply sprung from her as though she were another woman, a woman whose father hadn't abandoned her, whose brother hadn't beat her, whose husband hadn't cheated on her.

Just knowing that Alex had probably bedded many women should have made her nervous. In fact, she felt the opposite, quite comfortable. Well, as comfortable as a woman who hadn't kissed a man for five years could possibly be. They both knew the score. There was no romance involved. Just a prince and his private investigator pretending to be husband and wife.

Her kiss needn't do anything more than prove to them both that she could act like a wife in front of others. And it calmed her nerves to know that Alex had absolutely no interest in her as a woman. Since he would never want her, he was the perfect candidate for her to practice on. She could tilt her head back and reach his mouth with hers.

He was tall, but not too tall. Broad-chested in a natural way that made her think he'd look great in swim trunks. Or in a tuxedo. Or in a uniform.

He possessed a kind mouth with full lips that were slightly parted. Gathering her courage, she raised her mouth, taking care not to brush against him in any way, allowing only her lips to graze against his.

She was trembling so much she couldn't tell if he reacted to the touch of their lips. His expression didn't change and with his eyes closed, she felt almost anonymous. And oddly secure.

His lips were warm, surprisingly soft and pliant. With him standing so still, she took the opportunity to nibble and tease his bottom lip, exploring the slightly tangy taste of his mouth, breathing in a masculine scent that was distinctly his own.

"This isn't so bad," she murmured.

"If you'll allow me to hold you, I could show you bad," he teased, obviously already guessing at her answer since he didn't reach for her.

"I don't think so." His soft words had simply been a test, one she was determined to handle. "I think I'd rather just kiss you again."

"Be my guest." He didn't move, didn't open his eyes. "This time you might try opening your mouth."

"Why?"

"For a change of pace? For variety?"

She hesitated.

"You can back away whenever you wish," he coaxed.

She felt silly. She was a divorced woman, not some convent-bred virgin. She could kiss a man, especially one who had deliberately made himself as unthreatening as a statue.

Her ex-husband had been demanding, impatient, the sex stressful. But Alex's approach enticed her. He allowed her room to lightly explore the contours of his cheekbones, his jawline and the cords of muscles in his neck with her fingertips. She threaded her fingers through his blond hair, deliberately delaying another kiss.

"You are a tease," he told her.

"Was that a complaint?"

"A fact."

"You want me to stop?" she asked, surprised by

the silky texture of his hair, shocked that she was actually enjoying the give-and-take between them. Pleased that she was taking the first steps to putting her past behind her.

"I want...you to do...whatever you wish."

Wow. Talk about trust. Alex didn't know her. But then she realized that with a reputation such as his, he was probably bored by her timidity. At least he'd had the courtesy not to yawn or to make fun of her reluctance. She supposed he met women who dragged him into bed without a moment's hesitation. For a moment she wished she could be that kind of confident woman—not for him, but for herself.

She wished she could feel passion without fear, make love without hesitation. She wished she could explore without reservation, kiss without reluctance.

Where was her courage when she needed it? Alex was offering her whatever she wanted to take—no strings attached. And he had enough respect for her to allow her to make up her own mind. She shouldn't blow the opportunity.

She must be insane to hesitate. The man was a prince. He was gorgeous and rich. And completely at her disposal.

Surely she could acquire enough nerve to do more than lightly graze his mouth with hers?

She still hadn't decided what to do when a loud banging on the downstairs front door broke into her thoughts. In less than a second she stepped back from Alex, replaced her hand on her gun and turned toward the clamor.

Chapter Five

Alex fought past the roaring in his ears and battled his spinning senses. Taylor's erotic spell had not only entranced him, but had wrapped him in a silken web of desire that she'd woven as skillfully as any courtesan.

Opening his eyes, he blinked through the haze of passion she'd created by the mere brush of her lips on his and the slightest grazing of her fingertips over his face. She'd stunned him, evoking a reaction he'd never expected and couldn't rationalize. Although the shock had yet to wear off, he had to compose himself.

The incessant pounding downstairs hadn't let up, and Taylor was already out of the room and halfway down the steps. She'd flicked on the lights, allowing him to grab his stuff from where he'd tossed it on the bed, jam his hat on his head and don his sunglasses, grateful for the clear part of the lenses that allowed him to see in the dark. His disguise completed, he took the stairs three at a time.

He caught up with Taylor just as she opened the door. He noticed that she kept her hand in the pocket that held her gun and stepped directly between Alex and the intruder. She protected Alex with her life as casually as other women buttered their bread.

An embassy aide stood on the outside stoop. "Come quick. Bring your tools. There's a fire in the embassy and we think people are trapped."

Hoping he was up to fixing the problem, Alex picked up his tool belt and slung it around his waist, glad that the aide didn't see him fumble to buckle the stiff leather. In the process of donning the heavy tool belt, he dropped a screwdriver and bent to retrieve it.

Alex listened to Taylor question the aide. "How big is this fire?"

"It's contained on the second floor in one office."

"How far are the trapped people from the fire?"

"I'm not sure."

"Where exactly is the problem?" Alex asked.

"We think the fire's in General Vladimir's or the secretary of state's office. We've called the fire department. Right now the fire seems small, but if the sparks keep flaring, the entire embassy may go up in flames."

"Let's go." Alex picked up his tools and stepped past the aide, leaving Taylor to decide whether she was coming with them. He wasn't certain whether a gardener would follow her handyman husband into this kind of emergency, but he suspected that Taylor wouldn't stay behind.

She didn't hesitate, simply closing the door behind them. Without saying a word, she remained by his side, vigilant.

They hadn't gone fifteen meters—forty-five yards, he recalculated in American terms—before they turned a corner and spied spectacular flames shooting out a window. Devilish sparks glowed and hellish smoke billowed from curtains that had caught fire. The sprinkler system had quickly contained the flame but had the sparks caught elsewhere? The stench of burning fabric and scorched metal hurried his steps.

"Has anyone called the police or an ambulance?" Alex asked, hoping that help would arrive before he proved that he knew very little about his job. He could fake his way through small repairs, but this emergency seemed too big for even a qualified handyman to handle.

"We're hoping that won't be necessary," the aide replied. "General Vladimir fears a security breach and doesn't want foreigners inside our embassy. When the firemen arrive, he'll allow them to enter, but he claims that it's too easy for our enemies to use the emergency to insert a spy in our midst."

Great. And if the embassy burned to the ground, it would delay Nicholas's efforts to solidify his ties with the West. His big brother wouldn't be happy with another delay, wanting to consolidate support back home. But his first priority had to be to free the people trapped in the building before it burned to the ground.

When they entered the building, Alex was grateful for his hat, which protected him from the overhead sprinklers. His glasses fogged, but he didn't dare remove them and simply wiped his sleeve over the lenses. Inside, the burning smell mixed with the reek of damp carpets. Water squashed under his feet, causing him to wonder how long the sprinkler system had been on and why he hadn't been summoned sooner.

Taylor stuck closer to him than a shadow, her presence a constant reminder that they might not just be walking into a burning building with electrical problems to save people locked in an office, but into an ambush. Yet she hadn't hesitated and she'd done her best to remain inconspicuous. Just having her by his side gave him confidence.

Alex had fled this building during the night under horrific circumstances, leaving a wave of dead bodies behind. Returning and walking past the places where loyal men had died to protect him renewed his determination to save those trapped inside and to seek justice. But were tonight's problems caused by faulty construction, an accident, or something more sinister?

Between the lack of lighting and his steamy glasses, he was having difficulty seeing much in the dark hallway. Reaching for his tool belt, he found his flashlight on the third try and flicked it on. Water damage would be costly and set back the completion of the interior. At least the art had yet to be hung on the walls and most of the computer equipment hadn't been installed.

"Has the rest of the building been evacuated?" Taylor asked.

"Yes, ma'am. You might not want to stay. The sparking in the secretary of state's office was really terrible."

"I'm not leaving my husband alone," Taylor stated matter-of-factly.

"Is that where you are taking us?" Alex asked the aide. "To the trapped people?"

"You're supposed to break down the door and free them."

Alex frowned and made a quick decision. He hoped to stop the fire from spreading to the trapped people by the quickest means possible. "We need to shut off the electricity before we attempt to free them. Where's the breaker box?"

He might be the hired handyman, but he'd just arrived on the job this evening. Although he couldn't be expected to know the entire construction layout on his first day, it made perfect sense to shut off the electricity before breaking down the door.

"It's probably outside," Taylor muttered uneasily, clearly as suspicious of the aide as Alex was. Either the aide was ignorant of all things mechanical or he'd been ordered to lead them inside.

Keeping the aide in his sight, Alex swung down a hallway that led to the nearest exit. The aide should never have led them inside and, by following, he hoped they hadn't somehow jeopardized the lives of those trapped or walked into a trap themselves. He had an uneasy feeling, but realized that unless someone had already discovered his secret identity, he was being paranoid. Still, it paid to remain on guard. Although not many people were as intelligent and vigilant as his soon-to-be brother-in-law, if Hunter had figured out their scheme, others could do so, as well.

Once again outside the building in the smoky night air, Alex breathed a little easier. People had gathered around the front gate of the embassy to watch the smoke billow up from the building. At least he no longer saw the glow of flames or sparks, although they could flare up at any moment. Alex and Taylor hurried along a stone path bordered by a thick hedge.

He hadn't gone more than a hundred yards before he spotted the breaker box fastened to the wall. After lifting the gray lid, he shined the light inside and threw the main switch.

"Our security chief," the aide said, "will want a report about this." The aide left them to find Ira Hanuck, Chief of Palace Security.

Alex had known that eventually he'd have to test his disguise and come face-to-face with people who knew him well. He'd been hoping to put off a meeting until Ira had gotten used to seeing the handyman around the embassy before ever having to have a direct conversation with him. However, tonight's difficulties had moved up the timetable considerably.

Knowing she wouldn't remain behind, he led Taylor into the smoky building, determined to rescue the trapped people and to get out fast. Using the flashlight, he illuminated the walls and floor to get his bearings and spoke above the noise of the fire sprinklers and raining water.

"Look for a fire extinguisher," he directed, heading toward the stairwell that would lead to the burning offices.

As they moved deeper inside, the smoke thickened and he took Taylor's hand to avoid losing her. When she didn't immediately jerk away from his touch, instead allowing her hand to remain within his, satisfaction threaded through him. At least he had made progress on one front. She trusted him a little more than she had before.

"There." She pointed to an alcove with soda and snack machines. "A fire extinguisher."

He released her fingers and handed her the light. It took a moment to figure out the release mechanism. The extinguisher came free with a thump and proved heavier than he'd expected.

She shined the light on a metal label attached to the extinguisher. "It says—"

He didn't take the time to allow her to read the directions. The mechanism was simple enough. He snapped open the nozzle handle and pulled back the trigger. Foam sprayed, arching in front of them in a gratifying whoosh.

Leaving the vending area behind, they headed toward a stairwell that should take them upstairs to where the aide had said people were trapped. He reached for the doorknob, intending to enter the stairwell.

"Wait." She tugged him back. "Touch the door first to see if it's hot."

Good idea. He released her hand and did as she suggested. The metal door felt cool beneath his fingers, and he reclaimed her hand. "We can go on."

Emergency exit signs lit the stairs in an eerie glow, and with the dissipated smoke, it no longer seemed as though they were swimming through a viscous cloud. He expected the sprinklers to take care of the worst of the fire and hoped he could break down the door and free those who were trapped before any flames blazed up again.

Despite his hurry, before opening the second door

that led out of the stairwell, he paused to place his palm on the door to check for heat. "It's cool."

She tugged him back. "Stand back as far as you can, okay?"

He leaned forward, then shoved the door open with his foot. When no flames shot through, he used his arm to prop open the door and peek around it.

Here, the smoke was thicker than Turkish coffee. He could barely see two feet ahead. "Grab onto me. I don't want to lose you."

He took a quick, short breath, the acrid taste settling on his tongue, his lungs protesting with a series of coughs. He felt Taylor grab his shoulder strap where the material connected to the waist of his overalls.

His soaked clothes slowed his movements but added protection from stray sparks. Alex shuffled forward, peering through stinging eyes into the dark gloom. He heard the crackle of flames before he saw them and slowly blundered down the hall and through a doorway. With the smoke so thick, Alex didn't even know whose office he'd entered.

The sprinkler system seemed to have already doused the flames, leaving behind the stench of burned plastic, leather and rubber products. He eased one foot in front of the other, expecting to trip over furniture, a wastebasket or even a vacuum cleaner left behind by the cleaning crew. But the office appeared empty. Without exiting back into the hallway, he moved into the next office, advancing slowly, wondering why he heard no screams from those who were trapped.

He yelled. "Anyone here?"

No one answered. Were they already suffering from smoke inhalation and unconscious?

Taylor tugged on his overalls. "Fire." She coughed. "By the far wall."

The flames were neither bright nor hot, more like a flicker of yellow and orange in a black sea of fog. But as he approached, a gust of wind swirled the smoke and the flames hungrily licked toward them.

Alex depressed the lever on the fire extinguisher. Foam hissed out in a rush, smothering the flames. He stamped out stray sparks and prayed they were done. But as soon as one part of the fire died, another flame rose to take its place.

"We need a second extinguisher." She made the statement and let go of him at the same time.

"Don't go."

She paid no attention and the smoke swallowed her up. He debated turning back but the growing flames demanded his attention again.

A moment later he heard her scream.

TAYLOR BUMPED into someone. Someone who couldn't possibly be Alex. Someone silently skulking around in the dark. Powerful arms came around her, and she let out a shout.

"Are you hurt?" the stranger asked in Hungarian-accented English.

About to ram her knee into the man's groin, she delayed after hearing concern in his tone. "Who are you?"

"Chief of security, Ira Hanuck." His hands steadied her, then released her. Through the smoke she could barely make out more than his bulky silhouette. "Are you a secretary?" he asked. "I heard people were trapped up here and came to help. You need to vacate the building right away. It's not safe."

Well, duh! "We need another fire extinguisher."

"We?"

Alex shouted to Taylor. "Are you all right?"

"Yes, darling," Taylor told Alex, using the endearment to remind him they had to keep up their cover as husband and wife. Then she spoke to Ira, hitching her thumb over her shoulder. "My husband is putting out the flames back there so he can reach a door that is jammed. People may be trapped and he could use some help."

Ira bent and lifted a second fire extinguisher. "You should leave the building. I'll find him."

"I'll help you find him," Taylor insisted. "This way."

She led him back toward where she thought she'd left Alex. "Honey? Where are you?"

"By the window." He coughed, his voice sounding hoarse and raw.

Since she hadn't had to carry anything, she'd protected her lungs from the smoke by breathing through her shirt. Alex had been carrying the heavy extinguisher and hadn't had the luxury of straining air through his sleeve. He didn't sound good. On the one hand, he sounded nothing like he had earlier and the smoke in his lungs would help disguise his voice. On the other hand, severe smoke inhalation could put Alex in the hospital.

She and Ira followed a trail of foam and tromped through three singed and soggy offices before they caught up with Alex. Here, the flames were highest. In the brightness, she could see Alex's face smudged with soot. A perfect disguise—if he lived through the fire.

She wanted to tug him to safety, but he was clearly determined to reach the door behind the flames where she could hear someone pounding.

Oh, God. People really were trapped in there. All along she'd had doubts.

With Ira's help, the two men saturated the fire with foam. The sprinklers continued to rain down, soaking any stray sparks. Slowly, the men beat back the flames. They'd extinguished the last spark.

"Stand back!" Moments later, Alex used the fire extinguisher as a battering ram against the door. Nothing gave. He withdrew a screwdriver and removed the hinges while Ira stood guard with the extinguisher.

Finally the door clattered to the floor and two frightened women hurried out. Soaking wet, their clothes reeking of smoke, they appeared unharmed.

And then sirens screaming, the fire trucks arrived and men rushed toward the building with hoses and ladders.

Minutes later firemen helped the two women outside. Taylor peered out the window to the front gate where a heavy man with a thick Russian accent shouted at paramedics, refusing to allow them into the embassy. Any moment, she expected him to pull a weapon to keep back the police and paramedics.

Tired, out of adrenaline, Taylor shook her head at
the scene below. "The man's crazy."

"Who? General Vladimir?" Ira asked.

"Is he the one refusing to let the paramedics inside?" Taylor asked.

"Their presence is no longer necessary," Ira told
her.

"Flames could spark back up at any time. We need
to get out and let the firemen do their job," Taylor
said. She didn't understand these people. Security
precautions were one thing, but smoke inhalation
could kill them just as dead as terrorists. She had the
distinct feeling that both the security chief and the
general had something to hide. Could they be in ca-
hoots with one another?

She heard voices echoing down the hall and joined
Alex to present a united front to the strangers. Taylor
wasn't the least surprised to learn that the general and
another man had come up to survey the damage with
a group of firefighters.

Ira growled at both men. "What are you doing
here?"

"The fire started in my office," a wide-shouldered
man with a kind face answered gently. "Even this old
fisherman is curious about how the sparks started."

Taylor realized that the "fisherman" was Anton
Belosova, Vashmira's secretary of state and someone
Hunter had warned them about. She couldn't help liking the diplomat on sight. He had a kind face and
walked as if he carried the weight of his country's
future on his shoulders.

So far, none of the men had looked closely at Alex.

In his sodden clothes, with his hat pulled low and his face filthy from soot, she imagined he appeared nothing like the prince of Vashmira the three powerful men were accustomed to seeing. However, the sooner she and Alex left, the less chance the men would have of discovering Alex's identity.

She reached Alex's side and took his hand. "You should come breathe some fresh air, dear."

"Not yet." The general stopped them. "You're the new handyman, correct?"

"Yes, sir." Alex spoke hoarsely and Taylor suspected he didn't even have to disguise his voice. The smoke had taken care of that problem.

"Would you mind taking a quick look into Anton's office? I, too, am curious about the cause of the fire."

"My husband is not an arson investigator," Taylor protested. "Ask the firemen to help."

Alex headed into the office where the fire had started. "Won't hurt to look. Besides, we can't turn on the electricity until the wiring is checked."

"Tomorrow is soon enough," Taylor insisted. She wanted Alex out of here. Any of them could recognize him, and she had no idea how much he really knew about electrical wiring. With the water from the sprinklers still running, they all stood in puddles of water. She didn't need a degree in electrical engineering to know that any of them could easily be electrocuted if someone "accidentally" turned the main breaker switch back on.

"I'm okay," Alex insisted.

"You breathed in a lot of smoke. It won't take but five minutes—"

Alex pulled her into the secretary of state's office and flicked his light around the room. "We'll just take a quick look."

Why was he being so insistent on searching the place now? Did Alex think one of the men had come upstairs to hide the evidence of their arson?

Ira pointed to a dark black blotch on the wall. "By the look of that charred drywall, the fire burned hottest over there."

"Next to my desk," Anton murmured.

Alex knelt and shined his light on two wires. "I can't be sure, but these wires appear to be stripped."

"Stripped?" the general asked.

"Missing their insulation," a fireman who'd accompanied them explained. "If two stripped wires cross, they spark."

"Was this deliberate?" Anton asked Alex.

Alex shrugged. "I don't know, sir."

The fireman kneeled closer. "Could be arson. Could be an accident. It's difficult to say."

Ira frowned at the general and the secretary of state, ignoring Taylor and Alex. "We've just arrived. We hadn't even visited these offices. So there was no sensitive information—"

"I'm afraid there was." Anton sighed. "I sent file attachments ahead, so I would have the material when I arrived."

"What kind of attachments?" the general asked.

Anton hesitated, clearly he didn't want to speak in front of the gardener, the handyman and the fireman. "Political documents."

Taylor tugged on Alex. "I want the paramedics to check you out before they leave. Come on, honey."

Alex stood and she hoped this time she'd succeeded in convincing him to leave. He casually placed an arm over her shoulder, and she didn't mind at all. She just wanted to escape while their cover held.

But Alex wouldn't be hurried. "Sir, there's one other thing you might need to know."

"What?" the general asked with impatience.

"That locked office door?"

"Yes?"

"The lock was melted from the outside. As if someone had put a torch to it."

"You're saying those women were deliberately trapped," Taylor added. She watched the three men's faces carefully and decided she wouldn't want to play poker against any of them. They didn't reveal surprise. They didn't react at all. Would the sprinklers have put out the fire without the help from the extinguishers? It was almost as if they had expected that the fire had been deliberately started and that the arsonist had meant for the sprinklers to put it out before it went too far. But why?

Had someone stolen information from the secretary of state while the building was being evacuated and risked the lives of innocent secretaries to do it? That made no sense. If they'd been in Anton Belosova's office long enough to set a fire, they undoubtedly had had the opportunity to steal information then.

Four offices had been singed by the fire. Perhaps the arsonist had been interested in information from another office. Perhaps the fire had been a diversion to make it easier to steal something from another more closely guarded part of the building. Until she had the opportunity to speak privately with Alex, she couldn't even formulate her suspicions.

"Come, dear. I'm tired and tomorrow I have to fertilize the roses."

Alex hugged her to his side. "You were a big help."

Together they exited the offices and headed back to the stairwell, leaving the three men behind. As before, the smoke wasn't as strong here, and beside her Alex breathed in several large gulps of air.

"Do you think—" Alex began.

"Shh." Taylor slipped out from beneath his arm and placed her hand back on her weapon. "Did you hear that?"

"I can't hear anything with the sprinklers running," Alex complained.

As if the system had heard his statement, the water suddenly stopped. Either the sensors had kicked in or someone had turned the sprinklers off.

However, the ceiling continued to drip. Taylor heard a footstep and spun around and gasped as a silhouette emerged in the flickering light from above them. The security chief had followed them.

Ira spoke, keeping his voice low. "Glad I caught up with you folks."

"Why?" Taylor didn't like the way he'd sneaked up on them and her suspicions kicked in.

Ira reached into his pocket, took out several hundred dollar bills and offered them to Alex. "I have some special equipment I want you to install for me when you repair those walls.''

''What kind of equipment?'' Alex asked.

''Spy cameras.''

Chapter Six

Alex ignored the money that the security chief held out to him. "Spy cameras?"

Ira issued his order, almost as if he were talking to a moron. "Before the walls are repaired, I want you to install the fiber-optic wiring necessary to run mini Webcams."

Duh? Did the security chief think he would run the wires after the new drywall was up?

To keep the insult from showing on his face, Alex looked down at the hundred-dollar bills. "Sir, I'll need the funds for this to come through channels. Am I to understand—"

"You needn't understand. I'm authorizing the work and paying for the materials. What's to understand?"

At least the money wasn't a bribe. However, from Ira's annoyed tone, it was clear that Alex had overstepped the boundaries of his position by questioning the security chief. He wanted to ask if the chief would put his orders in writing but didn't want to raise the man's suspicions.

Without another word Alex accepted the money

and stuffed it into a soggy pocket. "It may take a few days—"

"The sooner the better," Ira told him before departing as quickly as he'd arrived.

In all his years at the palace, Ira had never spoken to Prince Alexander except with the most polite deference. Tonight, the man had revealed that Alex had never really known him. Sure, the security chief could have been worried about the fire, but that didn't excuse his rudeness. On the positive side, Alex now had a little more confidence in his disguise. The downside was that Ira might have sent someone to start the fire so he could install his cameras.

Taylor put her finger to her lips. Obviously she didn't want to discuss anything until they had more privacy. A smart idea, considering that they had no idea who had started the fire or why. And considering that the powerful chief of security kept appearing where Alex didn't expect him to be.

When Taylor led Alex out the front door toward waiting paramedics, she actually startled him. He'd thought her concern had been faked to separate him from the men who might recognize him. But she didn't hesitate to shoulder straight through the disbanding crowd of embassy workers, past the flashing lights of police cars to the large van marked Ambulance. Taylor seemed genuinely concerned about his health as she urged him toward the van, and then appeared relieved after the paramedics released him a few minutes later with a simple warning to go straight to the hospital if chest pains developed.

"I'm fine," he told her. "But I'd like to change out of these wet clothes."

"Me, too. Heck of a first day on the job," she told him as they strolled past several secretaries, obviously intent on keeping their pretence going.

He found the strain of remaining in character a challenge, interesting but damn annoying when he wanted to question his "superiors" and couldn't. At home, he routinely asked his aide to find out whatever he wished and had thought nothing of questioning people until they satisfied his curiosity, a perk he missed.

Yet, there were other perks to his new status. Alex found himself looking forward to his time alone with Taylor, whom he'd found more than willing to talk to him about possible explanations for the disturbing events occurring at the embassy. He wanted to hear her opinion of Ira's request, wondered what she'd thought about the handyman's acceptance of the cash and his agreement to install the cameras. Meanwhile, Alex hoped the Webcams came with installation instructions.

As he and Taylor walked up to the Victorian cottage, he increased his pace, eager to shed his wet garments, to take a hot shower and to order a drink.

Scratch the drink. Alex the Handyman wouldn't be ordering drinks from an aide or his valet for quite some time. His lower status would take some getting used to. Ah, but he would manage.

Taylor halted halfway across the cottage front yard. "We have company. Someone is on our stoop."

Noting their hesitation, the man stood. Alex recognized his brother's secretary of state, Anton Belosova, in the dim light. Anton held out his hands apologetically. "I know it's late, but I was hoping for a few minutes of your time."

Anton was just as polite to Alex the handyman as he was to Alex the prince. However, the diplomat's demeanor did nothing to ease the tension Alex felt radiating from Taylor.

She spoke cautiously. "Excuse me, sir. I don't believe we've met."

"I'm Anton Belosova, Vashmira's Secretary of State."

"Then you must be lost," Taylor told him. "This is the handyman's cottage. You'll want to go back to the main entrance, it's over—"

"I came to speak to you and your husband," Anton told her kindly but firmly.

"Is there a problem in your quarters?" Alex asked, hoping the smoke disguised his voice. It was rude not to invite Belosova inside, but Alex knew it was safer to remain outside where the darkness hid his features from the man who knew Prince Alexander so well.

Anton shook his head. "I'm sure my quarters are more than adequate. I'm a simple man, just a poor fisherman who has risen above his station."

"What can we do for you, sir?" Taylor asked.

"I need a favor." Anton shifted from foot to foot. When you repair the walls, I want you to secretly install security cameras."

Beside him, Taylor muffled a snort. He couldn't blame her. His countrymen sounded as if they spied on one another on a regular basis.

Alex folded his arms across his chest. "Why?"

"Because our country has a traitor, and I'm determined to catch him." Anton sat back on the step, took out a handkerchief and mopped his brow. "It's been a long night, but please bear with an old man. My wife betrayed everything I believed in when she attempted to assassinate our new queen."

"What?" Taylor gasped. "I have heard nothing..."

Alex supposed he should have told her the story, but there hadn't been time. Besides, he was curious to hear how Anton would speak about his personal tragedy. Despite Anton's long friendship with Alex's father and his continued work on Vashmira's behalf, Alex had never been completely convinced Anton was an innocent.

"King Nicholas kept the story quiet out of respect for me and my daughter, also to keep our country from suffering from a public scandal."

Taylor tensed, but removed her hand from her pocket and the weapon he knew she kept there. "I'm not sure how this has anything to do with my husband and myself."

"I cannot in good conscience ask someone to commit an illegal act without him knowing the reasons or the potential consequences for it."

"Go on," Alex told him. "We're listening."

"Before we were married, my wife hoped to marry King Zared the First. She failed to catch his eye, and she settled for me, an uncomplicated fisherman. To please her, I became a diplomat and have succeeded in serving my country—but I would have been content to remain a fisherman, especially after she disgraced..."

"Disgraced you?" Taylor prodded.

"My wife was also the mistress of General Vladimir for thirty years."

Taylor sat beside the man on the stoop. "I'm sorry."

"Perhaps her mind became twisted by her disappointment in me, but I never saw it. She took her own dreams and tried to force them on our innocent daughter. My wife plotted for Vashmira's new king to marry our Larissa. She attempted to kill the queen to clear the way for our daughter. When she was discovered, she threw herself down a well. She betrayed not just me, but our country, and for that I cannot forgive her."

Alex watched Taylor's face soften with compassion as they heard real pain in the secretary's voice, but he also heard the edge of anger.

"What does your story have to do with the illegal act you mentioned?" Alex prodded him back to their current situation, curious to hear the connection between his past and present circumstances.

"I have no proof, but I believe that General Vladimir influenced my wife's thinking, encouraged her to attempt to assassinate our new queen. That's why I'd like you to install a camera in his office to spy on the man. If I can catch him, I can repay my king for his continued faith in me."

And take his revenge on the man with whom he'd had to share his wife's favors for more than three

decades. Did Anton Belosova hate the general enough
to want revenge? How could he not?

But it could just as easily have been Anton who'd
sanctioned his wife's plotting. Perhaps Anton had encouraged his wife to go to the general. Perhaps husband and wife together had plotted for their offspring
to become the next queen.

Anton removed a roll of bills from his pocket.
"This is my own money. If it's not enough—"

Alex held up his hand. "Keep your money, sir."

Head high but shoulders slightly stooped, Anton
stood and brushed off his hands. "I'm sorry for taking
your time. I should never have asked you—"

"I didn't refuse," Alex said.

"Darling?" Taylor cocked her head in Alex's direction, her tone questioning his decision.

"I need to think," Alex answered.

Anton nodded. "One more thing. If you are caught
planting the extra security cameras, my government
will accuse you of spying. However, since you are an
American citizen and since my country wants to
deepen our relationship with the West, I believe the
worst that could happen is that you would lose your
position here."

Alex appreciated the man's honesty. "I'll let you
know tomorrow."

SCHEMES WITHIN SCHEMES. They trudged up the stairs
and Taylor wondered, not for the first time, if she was
in over her head. She didn't like operating in the dark,
didn't appreciate that Alex had failed to supply her
with information necessary to solving this case.

Not only was Taylor in the tough position of trying to keep Alex alive, but she was also pretending to be his wife, a role in which she was not comfortable. Wet, sooty and irritated, she didn't conceal her frustration. "How can you expect me to discover the traitor when you haven't told me more about the internal problems of your country?"

"I intended to fill you in," Alex replied reasonably. "We've been somewhat busy."

As if he needed to remind her. Most of her cases were slow and boring, involving hours and hours spent watching and waiting to catch a man cheating on his wife. But in this case, the action had been almost nonstop since Alex had first spoken to her. No wonder she was irritable, she needed space and time to think. But first she needed more facts.

"Are there any other assassination attempts you've neglected to tell me about?"

"Well, my little brothers were kidnapped last week."

"You're kidding?" She took one look at his serious face. His deep-blue eyes were hard and narrowed. "You aren't kidding." She breathed in and out but the tactic did nothing to calm her. "I didn't even know you *had* little brothers." She ran a hand through her wet hair and stopped on the stairs halfway up. "This isn't going to work. You need someone familiar with the backgrounds of—"

"I'll brief you."

Surely that couldn't be amusement in his tone, not with the danger surrounding his family. The one certain thing she'd learned about this man was that, however cavalier he appeared on the surface, he cared deeply for his family. Then she realized that he found her irritation with him amusing. The man had the oddest and seemingly inappropriate reactions, and sometimes she wondered if he deliberately used that touch of devilry just to distract her.

She countered by sticking to business. "Look, this case needs someone from Vashmira. Someone who understands how your system works."

He removed his sunglasses and stuck them into his pocket. In the darkness, his eyes remained enigmatic. Had she earlier imagined his amusement or had he switched tactics after realizing she intended to have a serious conversation? "Are you forgetting the generous fee I agreed to pay you?"

Yes. "No."

She had a reputation to maintain. Clients came to her because of her record, word of mouth in this city was better than placing an ad in the Yellow Pages. But even more important, she didn't easily accept failure, and she didn't see how she could possibly succeed when she didn't understand the dynamics, the interpersonal relationships and the politics in Vashmira. "Look, would you expect your generals to plan a war without proper intelligence?"

"I will fill you in," he promised with that oh, so charming look that had probably inveigled thousands of women into doing exactly what he wanted.

Damn it. She wasn't one of those women, and she resented that look, resented it down to her toes. Although the tiniest voice inside her admitted that it was agreeable to know he did realize she was of the female persuasion.

She really could use the fee he offered. And if she were successful, the case would probably receive publicity that could enhance her reputation. Plus, she'd already installed both of them undercover. To pull out now would hinder Alex. Besides, she wasn't a quitter.

"Tell me about your little brothers." She continued up the stairs. "I thought there was just Nicholas, Tashya and you?"

"Our mother died during my county's revolution. My father remarried about ten years ago. He and Sophia, his second wife, have three little boys. Dimitri is five, Nikita is three and Pavel is just seven months."

"And they were kidnapped?"

"The baby wasn't taken. We believe the kidnapper wanted to exchange the older boys for Tashya and me."

He believed? "You don't know?"

"Tashya and Hunter rescued the children. During the shooting, General Vladimir killed the kidnapper."

Funny how the general was the one man who hadn't approached them tonight. Didn't he need spy cameras, too? Alex had carefully made no judgments, giving her only the facts. So she could make her up own mind?

Yet something in his tone told her there was more. "And?"

"The kidnapper turned out to be the general's top aide."

They'd reached the bedroom, and she spun around

on her heel to face him. "First the general's mistress tries to kill the queen, then his aide kidnaps your half brothers and attempts to kill your sister. That's highly suspicious."

He nodded, a water droplet coasting through the soot on his aristocratic forehead down to his noble nose, spoiling his regal gesture. "But without the general's help during the revolution, our country would not be independent, and my father would never have been king. My father and my country owe this man a lot. And don't forget, the general did save my half brothers by shooting his aide."

Was he trying to convince her? Or himself? "Could he have shot his aide to keep the man from revealing where his orders came from?"

"Possibly."

From the way Alex answered, he'd clearly asked himself this question and had probably discussed it with his brother. Since he'd held back critical information she couldn't help wondering what else had he'd failed to tell her. "What I don't understand is the motive for all these assassination attempts. Why is someone trying to kill off your family?"

"We don't know."

"It seems to me that as the reigning king, Nicholas should be the primary target and that with him, you and your sister out of the picture, Sophia and her sons have the most to gain by your deaths. Could she be plotting with the general to put her sons on the throne?"

"Sophia and the general's aide were close before the man's death," he admitted.

"How close?"

"We thought he might have been trying to marry her, do away with everyone except the baby."

He hadn't exactly answered her question but she let it go, for now, intending to return to it, no matter how painful. She had enough sensitivity to respect his feelings, but not at the risk of his life.

Taylor moved on to other questions. "If the aide had eventually succeeded in killing the entire family except the baby and then married Sophia, he would have been the power behind the throne?"

"Yes. But since Nicholas's marriage to his American queen, the royal couple has been protected by your Secret Service. We believe the traitor is pursuing easier targets first. Like Tashya and me. After Nicholas and Ericka's wedding ceremony, someone shot at our carriage."

"What about Sophia? Could she have been plotting with the general's aide?"

"Maybe."

The briefness of his reply told her this was a tender point. He clearly liked his stepmother. "But?"

"Sophia's not the ambitious type."

Okay. She'd think about that later. She could understand how the idea of a conspiracy had only come to the royal family slowly. The assassination attempt on the queen had seemed like the plan of an insane woman intent on putting her daughter on the throne. The children's kidnapping and the attempted assassination of the princess seemed unrelated to earlier problems. But with this newest attempt to murder the prince, the events simply had to be related—but how?

Taylor suspected there was more she needed to know, but her brain could absorb just so many facts at one time. "I need a shower. We both do."

Alex opened the bedroom door and stepped back, his motion gallant. "You can go first."

She recalled from her earlier inspection of the house that there was only one full bathroom. The idea of sharing it with Alex, even assuming they would take turns, suddenly seemed too intimate. And to take off her clothes with him in the next room...no, she didn't think she could...

Alex must have read the misgivings in her expression. "You want me to go first?"

From the glint of humor in his eyes, she knew that he was teasing her, that he understood how uneasy she was. She had to give the man credit, he hadn't pried, and she probably owed him an explanation.

"I'm not real comfortable around men."

"I've noticed."

Again, no questions, just an easy acceptance and a step back to give her a little breathing room. The man could be amazingly perceptive when it suited him. Sometimes she had the feeling he was a master manipulator.

"If my past history is anything to go by, I should avoid the entire male race. My father abandoned our family when I was three. And my older brother..." She swallowed hard.

Alex's eyes burned with a cold blue flame. "He raped you?"

She shook her head. "He hit me. Not often but I never knew when he would vent his temper." And the fear of always wondering when and how her brother would strike out next was worse than the actual beatings. No one could understand the pressure of living with someone who could erupt at any time and for no reason unless they had experienced it.

Concern darkened his eyes. ''Why didn't your mother stop him?''

''He was five foot ten and two hundred and twenty pounds by the time he was sixteen. He hit Mom, too. Things were so strained at home that to get out, I married the first guy who looked at me. Three years later, I came home from working a double shift as a waitress to find my husband in bed with...another woman.'' The scene still gave her nightmares. ''At least I had the sense not to get pregnant.''

He winced. ''I'm not sure what to say except that all men aren't bastards.''

''My head keeps agreeing with you. But in my profession, all I see are cheaters. So, I'm just not that comfortable around men.''

''You want me to leave the house while you shower?'' he offered.

She paused a moment. Would she risk his life because she was uncomfortable? She couldn't envision this man barging through a closed door to get to her, not after he'd exhibited such masterful control of himself when he'd held still during their first kiss. Another man might have tried to go for more, but Alex hadn't pushed. Still, when she took off her clothes, she would feel safer with more space between them. ''Would you be insulted if I asked you to wait downstairs?''

"I could use a drink, and I think the bar had a half bottle of bourbon. Would you like a... What's the matter?"

"Nothing."

"What?"

Something about his worried gaze made her explain. "My brother used to drink before he..."

"Hit you?"

She nodded, unable to deny that the moment Alex had mentioned drinking bourbon, her stomach burned with acid. Guilt also stabbed her. First, she'd made him listen to her sad history, then she kicked him back downstairs in his wet clothes, and now she didn't want him to drink.

"It's okay," he said. "A soda might be better to quench my parched throat."

"Thank you." He really could act like a prince when it suited him. He hadn't complained, had simply offered to alter his behavior to set her mind at ease.

His voice softened. "You needn't thank me for simple courtesy."

"Where I come from, good manners are as rare as a sober man on payday. I may have left my old neighborhood, but some habits are difficult to lose, others are hard to change."

"Like never touching and kissing?"

Now why did he have to go getting personal again?

He leaned back against the balcony, the picture of gallantry, except for the gleaming light in his eyes that told her he was about to tease her. "Was kissing me so terrible?"

"I haven't thought about it much," she lied.

"Maybe you should kiss me again."

"Why?"

He chuckled. "I don't believe a woman has ever asked me that question. I'll have to think about it, but then maybe you should think about kissing me again, too."

His light tone did wonders in helping her stomach settle down. She thought he would stay and tease her some more, but he started to whistle a happy tune and headed down the stairs, his footsteps light, his movements graceful.

She should feel relieved. He'd gone downstairs. Told her he wouldn't drink alcohol.

She couldn't believe that his disappearance had left her slightly off kilter. Almost disappointed.

No, she had to be mistaken. She certainly couldn't be disappointed.

Taylor shut the bedroom door behind Alex to discover that the knob didn't have a lock. Neither did the one in the bathroom.

Chapter Seven

Vashmira

At the hum of his private fax, King Nicholas rolled out of the royal bed, careful not to disturb his bride. Vashmira's new queen still slept, weary from her new duties, especially from her tireless quest to help his sister convince the cabinet to enact laws on women's rights. Proud of both women, he had no doubt they would succeed, if not this year, then next. His concern ran in a different direction. The hours had dragged by in slow motion as he'd awaited word of Alex's fate.

Nicholas picked up a stiffly worded fax from Hunter, removed the paper key Hunter had given him and placed it on top of the innocuous letter.

Alex alive and well. Posing as embassy handyman married to P.I./gardener.

Yes! Alex had survived. Tremendous relief washed over Nicholas, and he sank to the window seat, the message still in hand. The good news seemed to drain the last of his strength, leaving a weakness in his knees and a thudding gladness in his heart.

Nicholas and his brother and sister had always been

close. During the year since their father's assassination, they'd grown closer. Many royal watchers often remarked on the differences between the two brothers, contrasting Nicholas's conscientiousness with Alexander's playfulness, but no one knew better than Nicholas how intelligent a mind was hidden behind Alex's playboy image. His brother, the equal of any professional commentator, could analyze Vashmiran politics with the keen understanding that Nicholas appreciated. And he was especially adept at figuring out puzzles. Nicholas was counting on his brother to help solve the problems facing them now.

Ericka, his new bride, awakened sleepy-eyed and came to him. "Good news?"

"The best. My brother's alive."

She sat next to him on the window seat and leaned into his chest. "I'm so glad. We should let your sister know the news."

"It's the middle of the night."

"Between worrying over Alex and Hunter, she's not sleeping much. I doubt we'll be waking her." Ericka hugged him, then rose to her feet, slipped on a robe and phoned Tashya's room, taking it upon herself to make the call.

"Be very discreet. The phone lines may still be tapped," Nicholas warned her. They needed to find the traitor soon. Living under this stress, in constant danger, had them all on edge. Worse, he needed to focus on the economy, on health care and on establishing a lasting peace with his neighbors—difficult to accomplish under the best conditions, almost impossible when under attack from someone within his own country.

Ericka must have been correct. Tashya arrived wide-awake in less than five minutes. Circles under her eyes revealed her lack of sleep. The moment she shut the door, the two women hugged, and Ericka told her that Alex was okay.

Tashya's eyes teared with happiness. "Thank you for telling me."

"There's more you might find of interest." Nicholas stood from his window seat, pleased the two women had become friends and unable to contain his amusement at the news he was about to impart. "Our brother is posing as the embassy handyman."

"A handyman?" Tashya's jaw dropped, and she used her hand to cover her open mouth. "Our Alex?"

Nicholas couldn't quite picture his elegant brother wearing anything but hand-tailored designer clothes, either. But he'd saved the most interesting part of Hunter's message for last. "Alexander's pretending to be married to a private investigator who's now pretending to be the embassy gardener."

"Oh, my." Ericka raised an eyebrow.

Tashya groaned. "Leave it to Alex to hide undercover with a woman. What did Hunter say about her?"

"Nothing."

"Nothing?" From his sister's tone, Nicholas judged that Hunter was going to have his hands full when he returned home. Then Tashya cocked her head and eyed Nicholas. "You have a way to contact my fiancé, don't you?"

Nicholas knew his sister's temper well and recognized her building anger. Obviously, Hunter hadn't given her a way to reach him and that Nicholas could, infuriated her. He attempted to mollify her. "For safety's sake, we have minimal communication. You don't want to put Hunter at risk, do you?"

Tashya didn't respond—unless he counted her fierce and possessive glare. Wisely, Ericka had learned not to take sides in these frequent family disputes. But Tashya only held back when it suited her. She scowled at Nicholas's fax machine. "You tell Hunter we want more information about the woman."

Nicholas might be king, but he didn't argue with Tashya. He was curious himself. Why had Alex sought the help of a female private investigator? Alex had never taken the threat to himself seriously. And knowing his brother, he had more than business in mind. Nicholas only hoped that Alex's attempt to combine business and pleasure didn't put his life in even greater jeopardy.

Washington, D.C.

HALF A WORLD AWAY, Alex paced in his wet overalls, the woman upstairs the primary focus of his thoughts. He didn't like the way he reacted to her big innocent eyes or the way he wanted to provide her with a feeling of safety more than he wanted to seduce her. He wasn't one of those men who felt inclined to protect women. In fact, he didn't believe women often needed saving. They tended to be strong creatures, much stronger than most men seemed to give them credit for.

Alex's usual pattern was to enjoy the chase, the conquest and then move on. Something had to be wrong with him because he felt differently about Taylor. When he should be moving forward, he found himself giving her additional room.

Sure, she'd had a rough life, but several women of his acquaintance had had equally or more difficult lives. However, those women had wanted him to save them. Taylor asked nothing for herself. He was sure she'd prefer him to stay away.

Her inner strength guided her, and he admired her independence, yet at the same time, he thought it might be nice if just once she needed him, leaned on him. Hell, at best, she had him confused and baffled by his own behavior.

If he held to pattern, he supposed the sooner he took her to bed, the sooner he would lose interest. Normally, he would be sharing that shower with his partner instead of walking around alone in wet clothing. Was that why he kept backing off? Maybe he didn't want to make love to her for fear of losing interest and then having to pretend that he still wanted her because they must continue working together. That would be a logical cause for his skittish behavior. This time he couldn't so easily move on.

If he'd had the luxury of a few drinks, he might have convinced himself of the validity of this argument. However, he was quite sober.

Not given much to self-analysis, Alex headed up the stairs when the pipes stopped singing, a sure signal that Taylor was finished and was probably dressing. He tried not to think about her night attire and hoped for flannel pajamas. Because after what she'd told him about her history, he'd feel warped for even attempting a seduction.

However, he saw absolutely nothing wrong with pushing her out of her comfort zone.

TAYLOR PREFERRED to avoid her issues about the male species. If possible, she would have expressly avoided facing up to her fears and insecurities during a case. But she'd accepted this case and now she found that none of the rooms besides the foyer and the master bedroom had furniture, as if someone had furnished two rooms and then run out of funds. She couldn't even relegate Alex to the proverbial too short sofa since there wasn't one.

During her shower she had tried not to think about the sleeping arrangements, or the heat in Alex's eyes, or the fact that she no longer found those hot glances quite so disturbing. She reminded herself that a man such as him was undoubtedly accustomed to having his every need catered to by willing women. Since she was currently the only female available, she supposed he might look to her.

Too damn bad. For him.

Taylor wouldn't be used by any man. Not ever again. She didn't care if the man happened to be the prince of Vashmira. She didn't care if Alexander was the sexiest man on the planet. She had flat-out made up her mind to protect her own interests. And those interests were to solve this case quickly, to collect her triple-net fee and to move on.

Except there was just the one bed.

Sleeping on the floor wasn't a good option. A restless night tossing on a hard floor when she needed to be alert tomorrow was not a good solution. And she could hardly ask His Royal Highness to sleep on the bare floor, either.

She towel-dried her hair and changed into her nightgown. She hadn't made up her mind what to do when she heard Alex's footsteps on the stairs. Although the gown covered her, she dived under the sheet and blanket, then scooted all the way to one side of the bed.

Before Alex knocked she called, "Come on in. The shower's all yours."

As he opened the bedroom door she clicked off the light. Since she'd left the bathroom door ajar and the light over the sink on, she could see Alex glance from the empty bathroom to the bed, his expression unreadable.

"I left you some hot water," she told him, hoping her voice sounded casual but fearing it might sound as tight as her ragged nerves.

"Hot water for tea?"

She restrained a nervous giggle. He'd probably never stayed anywhere less comfy than a five-star hotel. "Water tanks feed the shower. Sometimes the hot runs out."

"So you left me something hot?"

She hated it when he teased her and she had no

snappy comeback. "I have no idea how many gallons the water tank holds."

Well, now, that was clever, she thought sarcastically.

"If we're going to share that bed, a cold shower might be more appropriate."

He was teasing her again. She could tell by his light and breezy tone. She wished she had a suitably smart rejoinder that would reveal she intended to be an adult about the sleeping situation, but her tongue seemed molded to the roof of her mouth.

He plucked several items of clothing out from their purchases at the consignment store. "We didn't buy me any pajamas."

"Sorry."

"I usually sleep in the nude."

Damn him. She gritted her teeth until her jaw ached. Of course Mr. Playboy slept in the nude. But he wouldn't dare try that with her, would he? She didn't say a word. Didn't dare breathe. She simply reached under her pillow and placed her hand on her gun. She could see the headlines now: Frigid P.I. Shoots The Prince Of Vashmira's Royal Jewels. She had to bite down hard on her tongue to suppress another hysterical giggle.

Alex seemed totally unaware of her ragged nerves. He didn't seem to mind having a one-way conversation with himself, either. "However since we did buy one extra set of boxers, I suppose those will do."

She gasped in some air, realizing she needed to keep breathing when he teased her. Slowly she unclenched her fingers from around her gun, pried loose the weapon from her palm and told herself the man was teasing. Just teasing. She wouldn't overreact.

Except her stomach was doing backflips and her thoughts kept galloping out of control. As he showered, she told herself repeatedly that she could handle this case, but it didn't keep her mind from envisioning Alex, not ten feet away, naked, in a bathroom that they would share for the next week. Or thinking that after he finished, he would climb into this bed. With her.

Again, she reminded herself to breathe.

He took a long shower, and he whistled through most of it. She turned onto her side, facing away from him, and wondered if she could fool him into believing she'd fallen asleep. The moment he opened the bathroom door, she turned toward him, her hand slipping under her pillow. If there was danger coming, she intended to face it head-on.

His bare feet padded toward the bed and the covers rustled as he pulled them back. The entire mattress bounced as he rolled into bed. He fluffed the pillow behind his head and stared at the ceiling. "I've been thinking."

Really? Was now the moment when he'd decide they should make love? She had no doubt he'd have some very creative reason for her to consider.

"How good are you with computers?"

Computers? She'd been way off base. He hadn't been in that shower thinking up ways to convince her to have sex with him. He'd been thinking about the case, something she hadn't been doing enough of.

"Can you be a little more specific?" she asked.

"Hacking into the embassy—"

"Is way beyond my skills."

"But once we are inside the building, we have already bypassed the toughest security."

She frowned in the darkness. Had he deliberately turned the talk to the case to distract her from the fact that they were sharing the bed? If so, his tactic was working. Her stomach felt almost normal and Alex was lying shirtless less than two feet away. If she reached out her hand, she might brush against his bare side, so she made sure not to move even an inch in his direction.

She forced her thoughts back to the conversation. "Whose computer system do you want to hack into?"

"Anton's, Vladimir's and Ira's."

"You want to see what your secretary of state, your foremost military leader and your security chief are up to?" She scratched her head. "I might get into their systems, but Ira will probably know I was there. Or that someone was there," she amended.

"He wouldn't know it was us?"

"There are a handful of ways he might catch us."

"How?"

"With cameras hidden inside his office. Or, he could trace the prints I left on his keyboard, although I could wear gloves or wipe the keys clean. But he could simply walk in and catch us in his office. Unless…"

"What?"

"If the computers are on a network, I could send him an attachment to open that would give me access to his operating system."

"Huh?"

"I could override his password and get into his files undetected," she told him.

"What's the downside?"

"It's illegal."

"Even if we don't steal anything or do any damage?"

"I'm a private investigator, not an attorney. I try to obtain my evidence by legal means."

"You never go outside the law?"

"Do you?"

"In Vashmira, my family makes the law. The embassy is considered a tiny extension of home. We needn't worry."

"Unless he catches us and shoots us on the spot. Afterward he could claim he'd made a terrible mistake. With your disguise, he simply hadn't recognized you as the prince and everyone would believe him if he claimed he thought we were burglars."

"It's a chance we have to take."

TAYLOR APPEARED to relax as Alex spoke to her about the case. He risked moving his hand, deliberately allowing his knuckles to brush against her hip. Her response, an immediate jerk backward, had her scooting back so far that she almost fell off the bed.

"Sorry." He turned to look at her. "You aren't going to scream every time I turn over, are you?"

"I didn't scream," she replied tightly. "Are you going to install secret cameras for Anton and Ira?"

He allowed her to change the subject without comment. But he moved his foot, letting his toes skim her ankle. Again, she pulled back, but this time her re-action was calmer, and he took satisfaction that she'd lost a little of her wariness.

He considered her across the two feet that separated them. "What do you think I should do?"

"Well—" she punched her pillow, placed her cheek back down, and a lock of hair fell across her eye "—do you even know how to install that type of equipment?"

His fingers itched to push the hair back from her face. "Assume the cameras come with installation directions. Do you think I should honor their requests?"

"If you don't do the work, they'll find someone else who will." She spoke slowly, as if trying to figure out the ramifications before she committed herself. "And if you do the work, at least we'll know the camera locations."

Ever so slowly, slowly enough for her to read his intent and to withdraw if she wanted, he reached out and smoothed the hair from her eyes. He could have sworn she held her breath, but she didn't tell him to back off. She held perfectly still, doing nothing to avoid his touch.

"I assume you know where to purchase such equipment?" he asked, more interested in her tone than her answer. Was she still tense? Had his casual touch upset her? While he knew better than to hope she would enjoy the closeness between them, he hoped that eventually she would relax when she saw he meant her no harm.

"Yes."

Her one-word answer told him she remained uncomfortable but was undoubtedly working hard to conceal that emotion from him. At least she had the good sense to realize that her reactions weren't normal. Clearly, she was making a huge effort to overcome her past.

While he would have enjoyed coaxing her just a little further out from behind the fortified walls she had built, he wouldn't risk damaging the solid progress he'd made. Although he wanted to wrap himself around her and to sleep with her in his arms to prove he could hold her without pushing for lovemaking, she wasn't ready.

The conversation over, he slowly relaxed into a deep sleep.

When he awakened the next morning he found himself alone in the bed at the ungodly hour of five-thirty. Groggily, he calculated that they'd had less than four hours of sleep. Although Taylor had left the bedroom, she hadn't gone far. He could hear her light footsteps downstairs and smell fresh-brewed coffee.

Alex would have preferred to roll over and sleep until noon. However, even he knew that construction people arrived at work at the crack of dawn. He considered making a late entrance on his first day of work. He certainly could have used the fire last night as an excuse to grab a few more hours of sleep, but he didn't wish to call attention to himself.

With a groan, he flung back the covers. Ten minutes later he'd lost the boxers and was dressed in another set of ill-fitting overalls, a navy shirt with red lettering that read I Left My Cape At The Cleaners, and clean socks. Unfortunately, his only pair of sneakers still reeked of smoke from last night's fire. He had no choice but to wear them again.

If the morning hadn't come so early, if he'd been a little more awake, he'd probably have found some humor in his solitary pair of shoes. Back home, he had an entire closet filled just with footwear—custom, hand-sewn loafers made of the finest Cordovan leather, everything from wing-tip slip-ons to straight-tip Oxfords in a variety of colors and styles. One wall of his extensive closet was for sporting shoes, casual all-weather walkers and tassel suede moccasins, his English riding boots, designer sneakers, hiking boots, and slippers. And now he'd been reduced to one pair of smelly off-the-rack tennis shoes. Even his sister Tashya wouldn't believe he could manage with such meager belongings.

But manage he would.

When he entered the kitchen Taylor handed him a cup of black coffee, and he burned his tongue in his eagerness for a caffeine jolt. How she could look so wide awake and perky this early, he had no idea. She'd tied her hair back in a ponytail, and she wore jeans and a faded blue T-shirt that flattered her curves. A straw hat dangled from a cord around her neck and settled partway down her back.

He gulped more coffee. "Did you sleep?"

"A little."

Over the rim of his mug, he raised a questioning brow.

"Your snoring kept me awake," she teased.

He didn't snore. Too many women had assured him that he slept without uttering any noises, but he saw no reason to mention that. However, he did tend to toss and turn. And he loved to snuggle. He adored the differences between women's bodies and his own. He enjoyed their special scent, their soft skin and their heat that, mingled with his, created a cozy nest beneath the covers. He couldn't recall the last time he'd spent a night in bed with a woman and awakened to find himself alone. Instead, he usually found her pressed up against him, their legs intertwined. Had he, still asleep, reached out for Taylor during the night? He knew better than to ask.

"How do people do this every day?" he asked instead.

"Do what?"

"Get up while it's still dark."

"You're never up this early?"

"Not since the army, unless I didn't go to sleep that night," he answered.

She blushed. And he realized what he'd said. Damn. He hadn't meant to throw his experience at her. But he didn't think well before noon. However, he could cover up a mistake as well as any politician. "In the army, we often stayed up for forty-eight hours straight on forced marches."

"And then your valet tucked you in with a hot toddy and clean sheets?" She teased him again.

He groaned and held out his empty mug for more coffee. She pointed to the pot, and he poured himself another cup. "You want more?" he asked.

"No thanks. One cup is my limit."

"You do that a lot."

"What?"

"Set limits."

"And I suppose you never adhere to any, do you?" She spun around, leaned forward on the balls of her feet like a prize-fighter about to throw a punch. He took her aggression as a positive sign that she was beginning to feel comfortable around him. At least he hoped so.

"Easy." He held up one hand. "It's too early in the morning for sparring practice."

She grinned. "Oh, really. You don't want me to use you for a punching bag?"

He groaned. "Let me guess. You're a black belt—"

"Brown belt."

"—in karate?"

"Judo. It's the martial art of self-defense."

When he really woke up, probably after finishing his second cup, he'd have to remind himself she could probably throw him across the room. "What does that mean, exactly?"

"Judo was developed to use one's opponent's aggression against him."

"Is that another way of saying that the bigger the foe, the harder he falls?"

She shrugged daintily, amusement in her eyes. "Something like that."

Chapter Eight

Taylor enjoyed teasing Alex. She liked the way she felt about herself when she was with him. While she might not be at ease with the glimmer of his smile or the gleam in his eyes, she no longer felt so uncomfortable. And he didn't seem to have a temper.

On the walk from the cottage to the embassy, she realized that she wouldn't have minded if he had taken her hand. While it occurred to her that she could reach out and take his, she didn't feel *that* comfortable. And she wasn't going to push her luck. However, she did look forward to spending another day with him and had begun to think they could make a good team.

Early morning's first rays of pink slashed against the purplish sky, and she took stock of the activity around the embassy. Men in suits and ties, ladies in blouses and skirts and smart-looking shoes entered the building through the double front doors. Even from here, Taylor could hear the street traffic starting to jam up. Through the open gate she saw pedestrians walking their dogs and heard several impatient drivers honking their horns.

The Vashmiran embassy grounds encompassed the northern third of the block. Surrounded by high walls with thick hedges, the only way in and out appeared to be through the main gates where two on-duty guards stood on alert, checking identifications and waving people and vehicles through.

While Taylor was supposed to be the gardener, the grass, flowers and hedges would have to wait. She had no intention of leaving Alex alone. "If anyone asks, I'm staying with you today to help out with the carpentry. After the fire, the construction schedule must be further behind, so I don't think anyone will question my presence as your helper."

Several members of the cleaning crew came out a side exit for a cigarette break, and Alex slipped back into his undercover mode with the ease of a chameleon. He sipped his coffee, his tone light. "You don't want to let me out of your sight, do you, sweetheart? After all the years we've been married, I thought you might be getting tired of me."

Sweetheart? The endearment rolled off his lips with such practiced ease that she wondered how often he'd used it. "We've only been married two years, three months and five days."

"In my family that's a record." Alex hooked his arm through hers. At the same time he bent his head and whispered, "There's someone in the shadows by those trash cans."

She narrowed her eyes. "Am I mistaken, or is that the general?"

"That's Vladimir, all right." Alex tilted his hat

lower over his forehead and slipped on his sunglasses. "What's he doing?"

"Taking out his trash?"

"General Levsky Vladimir, hero of the revolution and supreme commander of Vashmiran forces, doesn't take out the trash." Alex strolled over to the Dumpster. "Morning, sir. We're going to start repairs on the damaged offices today. Any requests?"

The general frowned at Alex and Taylor. In the dawn light, reading his expression wasn't easy. He appeared more annoyed than upset by their interruption. "Those fools who put out the fire shot foam all over the embassy."

"We'll clean up the mess," Taylor told him cheerfully.

The general threw his hands into the air. "I'm surrounded by fools."

"Excuse me, sir?" Alex questioned the man.

The general just shook his head, muttered, "Fools," and headed back toward the embassy.

Taylor scratched her head. "Strange man. Is he always like that?"

"Like what?"

"Disgruntled?"

Alex shrugged. "I'm surprised he spoke to us at all. It was too much to hope he'd explain himself, but didn't it appear to you that he was looking for something in the container?"

"You saw him before I did. What made you think that?"

Alex waited until the general entered the embassy, then he quickly turned and headed back to the trash.

"I didn't see him throw anything in there, and he was leaning forward and peering down."

"What are you doing?" Taylor asked.

"I want to see what he was looking at."

Taylor looked back over her shoulder. "This isn't a good idea. Suppose he comes back out? Suppose he's watching us through a window?"

Alex plucked two soda cans out of the trash. "I'll tell him that we recycle."

Taylor sighed. While she didn't want Alex to do anything suspicious, if they always took the safe course, they would never learn anything. While he peered at the trash, she kept careful watch.

No one seemed to pay them any attention. The cleaning crews had ended their break and headed inside. Overhead in the large oaks, a few squirrels made impossibly long leaps from branch to branch. The guards at the front gate remained busy with their duties.

Everything appeared normal. But Taylor's neck prickled. She didn't like Alex putting himself at risk. "See anything interesting?"

He reached into the container. "Here's a half-burned legal pad. And several computer disks. The rest of the papers are shredded."

"Let's get out of here."

"I'm with you." Alex stuffed the disks into his pocket and tucked the legal pad under his arm so that only the unburned part stuck out. "We're supposed to report to the administrator's office. It's on the ground floor in the rear of the building."

They walked into chaos. Phones rang faster than

the secretaries could answer them. A messenger boy literally ran right past them. Mail to and from Vashmira stood in sacks, waiting for delivery.

Alex glanced at an empty cubicle with a computer.

"Don't even think of trying to look at those disks now," Taylor snapped at him.

Alex nudged her closer to the empty booth where a clipboard hung from the wall. "That's the list of whoever called in sick today."

"So?"

"If you started the fire, would you show up for work?"

"Damn right I would—to avoid suspicion."

"But suppose you got paid off? Would you work then?"

Alex took out a pen and wrote down the names of three people who'd called in sick. Taylor just knew they were going to get caught. The room was busy, but not so busy they wouldn't be noticed. Alex was just replacing the clipboard when a harried-looking gray-haired man hurried over. His name tag proclaimed him the administrative officer, Peter Kleg. "Just what in hell are you doing?"

"Searching for my work schedule," Alex replied, calmly straightening the tilted clipboard and making no effort to hide his interest in what had been written there.

Kleg frowned at Alex. "That's the list of people out sick."

"I see that. Now. Perhaps you could direct me to the—"

The officious man raised his voice and held out his

hand, palm up. "Let me see your embassy identification."

"Sure." Alex handed over the ID. "I guess after the fire last night, everyone's a little edgy."

Kleg didn't answer, and Taylor hoped he wouldn't demand that Alex remove his sunglasses to match his face to the picture—a picture that deliberately showed Alex with red-eye from the camera's flash. When Kleg simply handed back Alex's identification and peered just as suspiciously at Taylor's, she forced her shoulders to relax. With a tight nod, Kleg appeared satisfied. "Come with me."

They followed him through a corridor, past offices where the embassy replaced stolen and lost Vashmiran passports and issued emergency funds to their citizens and past another office where they kept track of the births and deaths of Vashmiran citizens in the United States. Then, Kleg led them by the visa office and into a controlled access area where a guard checked their identification once again.

Taylor had expected the chief administrator to be busy, especially after last night's fire, but Kleg's office was a zoo. Stacked boxes of documents, file folders and policy manuals covered every available table and desk surface, then overflowed onto the floor. Faxes spit out documents and phones rang. Kleg ignored the commotion and headed straight for one of his three secretaries.

When the woman didn't look up fast enough from her typing, he rudely snapped his fingers. "Mol, I need the work order for the new handyman."

"It's not ready."

"What do you mean, it's not ready?"

"You authorized the work order before the fire. You can't expect a man to paint walls that no longer exist," the secretary pointed out.

Kleg rubbed his forehead and spoke over his shoulder to Alex. "Look, maybe you should come back next week."

Taylor exchanged a glance with Alex, who shook his head slightly, indicating he didn't want to leave the premises. She didn't blame him. They had to conduct their investigation inside the embassy.

Help came from an unexpected source. The secretary sighed but kept her tone polite as she spoke to Kleg. "You're going to send the handyman away when you need all the help you can find to get this embassy ready for King Nicholas's arrival next week?" Behind Kleg's back, his secretary rolled her eyes at the ceiling. "I'm sure they can see for themselves what needs doing and make themselves useful."

"Yes, ma'am." Alex nodded. "Where do I request purchase orders for supplies?"

The able secretary went over operating procedures, and Kleg left. Taylor wondered if the secretary ran the office. She seemed much more capable than her boss.

On their way up to the offices where the fire had done the most damage, Alex seemed especially quiet. Pensive.

"Anything wrong?" Taylor asked.

"I'm sure getting a different perspective on this embassy and how it's run."

"When you're at the top, everyone sucks up to you, huh?"

"Mmm."

Alex couldn't answer as they walked by a group of carpet cleaners. Taylor and Alex took the stairs to the next floor, and, immediately, the stench from the fire hit them. But after a few minutes Taylor's nose seemed to burn out and she actually got used to the smell. However, she found the sawing and hammering of the carpenters not only nerve-racking but slightly alarming, as it drowned out the sounds that would warn her of the approach of strangers. So she kept watch with special vigilance, turning casually so she could look in all directions.

What remained of the carpet and padding had already been torn out. The carpenters had finished tearing down several burned walls and were already hammering in new studs. An electrician stood on a ladder, his head inside an opening that would eventually encase lighting.

Alex took Taylor's hand and tugged her down the corridor and into one of the undamaged, empty offices. The room could use a fresh coat of paint to cover the smoke damage, but the desk and computer system appeared to be newly replaced and in working order.

Alex flipped on the computer. While they waited for the operating system to boot, he reached into his pocket and retrieved the computer disks he'd filched from the trash. He popped one into the computer's floppy drive.

Using the mouse, he clicked File, searched for the

A drive and then brought up the disk's contents. "It's empty."

"Try another one," Taylor suggested as she kept a lookout in the doorway. No one seemed to notice them. The crews were too busy with their assigned tasks. Additional men carried in supplies of window frames and doors, hinges and knobs, cabinets and mirrors, and even a water cooler awaited installation by a plumber.

Alex put in the second disk. "This one has data on it."

"Anything interesting?"

"Lots of e-mail from one of the people out sick, a Mark Willard. Too much to read right now." He ejected the disk and replaced it in his pocket. He'd just popped the last disk into the drive when the security chief stepped out of the stairwell and headed toward the construction crews.

Just his presence on this floor made Taylor edgy. "Ira's inspecting the progress. Hurry. He could come this way."

"Almost done."

Taylor glanced over her shoulder at the monitor. She could see a long list of files on the last disk. "Anything interesting?"

"Maybe."

Alex kept that disk, too. He rose from the desk and joined her. They'd taken just a few steps toward the offices when Ira reappeared. When he spied Alex and Taylor, he jerked his head toward another empty office, indicating that he wanted another private conversation.

Taylor wondered if the security chief intended to question what they were doing at this end of the building or why the gardener wasn't outside gardening. Instead he shut the door behind them with a firm thud. "What was so interesting in the trash?"

"Excuse me?" Taylor stalled for time, her nerves ragged and as jumpy as oil on a hot skillet. Had the security chief seen them with the general? Had he seen them take the disks from the Dumpster?

"All papers that leave these offices are shredded. But I saw you—" he spoke to Alex "—take a pad out of the trash."

Taylor prayed he didn't know about the disks.

Alex took out the pad from his tool satchel and handed it to Ira. "We recycle. There's nothing written on those pages, but if we've somehow violated your security protocol, I apologize."

"Pretty fancy vocabulary for a handyman," Ira commented, taking the pad and flipping through the pages while Taylor held her breath, hoping there wasn't something written on those pages that they simply hadn't yet found.

Alex shrugged. "Not everyone has a rich father who can send them to college. Some of us have to work our way through. And I'm studying to take my contractor's test. I intend to have my own firm one day."

Taylor thought Alex had recovered quite well. Instead of attempting to deny his inappropriate vocabulary, he'd made a reasonable explanation for it.

Ira nodded and handed back the empty pad of paper. "You're ambitious."

"Industrious," Alex countered. "Industrious enough to have already ordered the specialized equipment you requested. We're expecting delivery this afternoon."

"When will you complete the installation?" Ira asked, his tone impatient.

Taylor knew Alex had no idea. But he sounded as if he knew exactly what to do and as if he'd done thousands of similar jobs. "Sir, that depends on the carpenters and the electrician."

Ira clapped him on the shoulder. "Keep me informed."

Moments after Ira's departure, Taylor sagged in relief. While she no longer expected anyone to penetrate Alex's disguise, she couldn't relax. Not when so many things could go wrong. Not when she had no idea who was after Alex or why.

ALEX FELT a number of undercurrents running through the embassy that came down from Vashmira's top brass. And during the afternoon the security chief, the general and the secretary of state all found reasons to inspect the construction progress. After crews tore away the singed drywall and checked for stud damage, Alex ran the wiring for the security cameras that both Ira and the secretary of state had requested. No one seemed to notice or question his work, and he didn't even try to be secretive.

One of the electricians had lent a hand when the procedure turned technical. Pleasure zinged through Alex when he tested the fiber-optic system and his results showed up on a computer screen thanks to dozens of miniature cameras. He'd hidden a multitude of the tiny cameras that were less than an eighth of an inch in diameter in the juncture where the walls met the ceiling, in molding joints and in the lighting fixtures. From Ira's office, Alex could bring up a clear view of both the secretary of state's and the general's offices. And from the security chief's office he could spy on the general and the secretary of state. With almost everyone spying on everyone, Alex figured they were all better protected.

While he had computer access, he removed Mark Willard's e-mail disk from his pocket and inserted it into the floppy drive. The man had never shown up for work today, but as Taylor had pointed out, his absence didn't make him guilty of arson.

Alex frowned at the large file. ''There are sixty pages of e-mails on this disk.''

''Why don't you search for General Vladimir, Anton Belosova and Ira Hanuck to see if anything pops up,'' she suggested. ''Do we know this Mark Willard's position at the embassy?''

''He's an aide to the chief of protocol.''

''Which means?''

''He has access everywhere and to everyone. His security clearance is high. He has to brief our staff when they meet their foreign counterparts. He knows what the delicate issues are and who must deal with those issues.''

''What possible motive could he have to set the fire?'' Taylor asked.

''He could have absolutely no reason to commit arson, but have been paid by someone who does have a motive. Or Mr. Willard could be working for one of Vashmira's neighbors who aren't keen on my country's attempt to strengthen diplomatic ties to yours. Or he could be a pyromaniac.''

''And have no reason at all?'' She shook her head. ''That I don't buy. Whoever is running this operation against your family has thought out their attack with care. To keep the heat off themselves, they've made the other attempts on your family appear to be the work of individuals. And when those individuals failed, your nemesis carefully covered his tracks.''

''Here's correspondence from General Vladimir, but it looks innocent enough.'' Alex skimmed a note from the general that confirmed his meeting with Pentagon officials in another few days. There were two more e-mails from the general, one about security precautions and the other asking about the embassy's construction progress.

''Do you think it odd we saw the general around the Dumpster this morning and here is his name on the file?''

''Maybe. But there's nothing odd about the e-mails.''

''Anything between Willard and Anton or Ira?'' Taylor asked.

Alex did another search. ''Nothing with Ira. But Anton wrote Willard that the secretary of state's office would approve the funds for extra equipment, which is a little outside Anton's normal domain.''

She peered over Alex's shoulder to read the screen. ''What kind of equipment?''

''The message doesn't say.'' Alex restrained a sigh.

It would have been useful to have Willard's correspondence to Vashmira, not just the replies. "I want to speak to this Willard, see if he's really sick."

They returned to the cottage, took hasty showers and changed clothes, a necessity after their laborious work day. Alex frowned at his smoke-stenched sneakers, then tried not to think about wearing them again.

When they headed back out, Alex's stomach rumbled. He hoped they could eat along the way. Physical activity always left him with an appetite.

"You have an apartment address for Mark Willard?" Taylor asked him, digging into her pocket for the keys, then locking the front door behind them.

"I found his address on the Internet." He handed her the directions and noted that she'd kept the keys in hand. "Do we need your car?"

She glanced at the address and nodded. "It's about a half hour drive. Do you think we should call first to find out if Willard's home?"

"I'd rather surprise him."

"While you showered, I used my cell phone to ask a friend to check out Mark Willard's background. Except for three speeding tickets, he's never had a problem with the law. He attended college, majoring in foreign languages. He's fluent in Russian, English and Hungarian."

"Is he married?" Alex asked.

"Nope. Why?"

Taylor had worked beside him all day, reeling out the fiber-optic wiring, helping tuck it between the wall studs, and all the time keeping her eyes open for anything suspicious. He'd made it a point to touch her throughout the day—just casually, when he handed her a hammer or when he pulled up a chair for her to sit beside him to test the system.

She no longer jumped when he brushed against her, although sometimes her eyes flared with uncertainty, as if she knew exactly what he was doing and couldn't make up her mind how she felt about his actions.

"I'm just curious about Willard." Alex wasn't as suspicious about the other two absentees. Neither held such high-level positions that they had free access throughout the embassy. "I wish we could check Willard's bank account to see if he's made any large deposits recently."

She hesitated. "Let's check him out first."

Alex didn't press her. In Vashmira, he could have had an answer within minutes with a simple phone call, but the United States had much stricter privacy laws to protect the banks and their customers. Unfortunately, those same laws also protected criminals.

Taylor unlocked her car and drove out of the parking lot. Three cars followed them and all were forced to turn right onto a one-way road that was four lanes wide and overloaded with bumper-to-bumper traffic.

Alex glanced at the clock on the dash. Six o'clock; they'd been caught in rush-hour traffic.

Taylor seemed in no hurry. She drove with more patience than he could have shown. Alex leaned back and appreciated her competent hands on the wheel, her smooth working of the gas and brake. Her coordinated, polished and professional efforts led him to believe he couldn't have placed himself in better hands.

Oh, yeah. He'd like to be in her hands all right. Not that she had any intention of complying with his lusty wish. Taylor had built her protective walls strong and high. As much as he wanted to use a battering ram to tear down the sturdy bricks she hid behind, doing so would just cause her to flee.

So he'd be patient, chipping away at the cracks, satisfying himself that sometimes a brick occasionally fell and he'd glimpse a view of the passionate woman she'd hidden. However, he meant to kiss her again. Very soon. The thought of actually holding her in his arms while he kissed her enticed him, teasing his senses like the promise of rain after a long drought.

Taylor turned right; her eyes checked her rearview mirror. Ten seconds later she rechecked it and frowned.

"Is there a problem?" he asked.

"The silver sedan with the dark-tinted windows is following us."

Chapter Nine

"What do you want to do?" Alex asked her. Muscles tensed, he was as edgy as a panther about to spring on prey.

Alarmed, but not panicked, Taylor kept driving, considering their options. "We could use my cell phone to call the cops."

"That probably won't solve anything. It's not illegal to tail us."

"True. I could circle 'round, and we could try to get a license plate number and have the registration traced. Or I could stop and confront the driver."

"No."

While she didn't want to attempt any heroics, she wondered what Alex was thinking. It was unlike him to make such a hasty decision without giving an explanation. However, this time, she didn't want to hear his reasoning. His adamant *no* had sounded personal, as if he was worried about her safety. While she appreciated the thought, she wouldn't allow his concern for her to get in the way of her work.

And since she agreed with him that stopping wasn't a good option, she simply gave him another choice.

"I could attempt to lose the tail, but that would let them know we've spotted them and possibly give away our cover."

"I suppose you're right. It's unlikely that a handyman and a gardener would recognize a tail."

Taylor kept driving, searching for the right traffic conditions. As they moved away from the downtown area, the traffic had lightened somewhat. When a light ahead turned yellow and normally she would have stopped, she stepped on the gas, speeding through the intersection. "Our tail caught the red light. If I make a few turns, they may just think they lost us due to bad luck."

As Taylor turned down side streets in a seemingly random pattern, Alex kept watch behind them. But Taylor spotted the silver sedan first. "They're ahead of us. Waiting. Almost as if they…"

"Almost as if they what?"

"Have a tracking device attached to my car."

"Would that mean they know who I am?"

"Not necessarily. The precaution might be standard procedure after all the trouble at the embassy. I just wish we knew who was in that car."

"If you stopped our vehicle and we searched under the hood and the chassis, could we find the device?"

"Maybe. Why?"

"If we removed it and put it on another vehicle, then our tail would follow the wrong vehicle."

Taylor shook her head. "It's a good idea except I'm not sure we have time to stop. And again, do we want to alert the tail that we know they're following us?"

"What do you suggest?"

"Why don't I try to lose them again? Then we ditch the car and take public transportation."

Her scheme might work. Their pursuers wouldn't know for sure that Alex and she had spotted the tail or why they'd abandoned the car, and so they would have no reason to question Alex's identity. Of course, they might already know his real identity, hence the tracking device.

Taylor took advantage of a funeral procession this time, then followed signs to a mall parking lot. They strode through the mall, bought chicken nuggets and lemonade, then sat on a bench to wait for a bus while they ate.

While Taylor asked some of their fellow passengers, who also waited for the bus, about schedules and routes, Alex simply sat back and watched her from behind his sunglasses. The man seemed to find many of her actions amusing, which irritated her more than she wanted to admit.

While they had been walking through the mall, he had casually placed an arm across her shoulders. She'd thought about shrugging out from underneath his touch, but had decided they shouldn't risk calling any attention to themselves. Besides, she hadn't minded so much.

Flirting seemed so much a part of Alex's nature, she figured his actions meant nothing. And since his gesture meant nothing to him, she refused to reveal by shrugging him off that it meant something to her.

When she recalled their kiss, she realized that he wanted more from her than she wanted to give, but she also knew that he would settle for whatever she was willing to give. Alex might coax, but he never insisted. He gave her room to make her own choices. Just knowing she had the freedom to pull away any-time had given her the courage to allow his arm to stay around her.

For several moments she'd even allowed herself to believe she was simply walking through the mall with a handsome man. However, her thoughts kept return-ing to the tail they'd picked up from the embassy. Had the driver found their car, which was parked out-side in the lot? Would their pursuer attempt to follow them into the mall, or just wait until they went back to the car?

Finally, their bus arrived and they found seats up front. Taylor consulted the driver about the schedule for the return route, then settled back in her seat. She couldn't quite relax and for the next ten minutes kept an eye on the road, looking for the silver sedan.

Alex seemed to sense the moment she concluded that they'd made a clean getaway. "Remind me not to give you a reason to run away from me."

He was back to teasing her, but she didn't mind. In fact, his good humor helped keep the tension from wearing her down. As much as she would have pre-ferred to stay at full alert, her body demanded rest between the spurts of adrenaline that were so much a part of this job.

"I wish we could both go on the run and disappear. At least you'd be safer," she told him.

"My goal isn't my own personal safety," he re-minded her, his tone even. "We need to find out—"

"Who is after your entire family." She again glanced over her shoulder at the road behind them. "We might have made a mistake—not checking out those men, but I have a feeling they'll be waiting for us when we pick up my car. Maybe we'll try to sneak up on them, get close enough to have a friend of mine run the license plates."

"But first we talk to Willard?"

"Yes."

Willard lived in a large, gated apartment complex. To drive in took a security code. Taylor and Alex struck up a conversation with a tenant walking his dog, and the guard assumed they were all together and waved them through.

Three wrong turns and several staircases later, Taylor pressed the buzzer on Willard's third-floor apartment.

"Go away," sobbed a female voice from the other side of the door.

"We're looking for Mark Willard." Taylor spoke loudly so her words would carry through the door.

"That S.O.B. doesn't live here anymore."

Alex and Taylor exchanged a look. She took a deep breath and tried again.

"Ma'am, can you tell me where he lives now?" Taylor asked.

"Lady, you don't want him. Believe me." A tiny brunette opened the door, revealing a black eye, a cut lip and a multitude of bruises. Self-conscious, she held together the ripped shoulder of her dress.

Taylor restrained a wince. The woman's battered face brought back an onslaught of fears and frustrations and memories of her own helplessness at her brother's hands that she'd done her best to repress. ''Did Willard do that? Do you want us to call the police?''

''Are you all right, ma'am?'' Alex asked gently.

While Taylor practically panicked at the all too familiar pervasive feelings of fear and defenselessness, Alex strode into the apartment and headed straight for the kitchen. He opened the freezer, cracked ice out of a tray and wrapped it in a dishrag while the stunned woman watched him with suspicion.

''What are you doing?'' the woman asked, fear and distrust in her eyes.

Alex returned and offered her the ice pack. ''This will help keep down the swelling.'' Without touching the woman, he led her to the sofa and gestured for her to have a seat.

Taylor trailed behind them. Her stomach rolled with nausea. Wherever she looked in the tiny room, her eyes met with the results of violence. The broken picture frames, the tipped-over chair and several broken dishes portrayed all too clearly that once again a man had lost his temper and taken out his rage on a woman.

Taylor reminded herself that she was no longer helpless. She had a permit to carry a deadly weapon and possessed the skill to use it. She'd also spent years in the gym, learning how to defend herself with her bare hands against stronger opponents. She was no longer the child that her brother had beaten. No longer the woman that her husband had cheated on.

So why couldn't she rid herself of the bitter taste of fear, of dread, of wanting to hide?

"What's your name?" Alex asked the woman with a tenderness and courtesy that tugged at Taylor. She knew Alex well enough to recognize his outrage, yet he was doing what he could to allow this woman her dignity.

"Donna. Donna Willard."

"We're from the embassy," Alex explained, "and here to check up on your husband's absence from work today."

"He was fired," Donna sobbed.

Mark Willard had not only beat his wife, he'd lied to her. Willard would not have been on the absentee list if he'd been fired. Had his supposed firing been his excuse to hit his wife? Taylor shook her head. Most abusers didn't need an excuse to lash out. In their sick minds, the woman always deserved the beating.

"Do you know where he went?" Alex asked without anger. But Taylor knew the effort it cost, saw him flex his fingers into a fist and then release them.

"You can't send the police after Mark," Donna insisted, her tone rising in panic.

Alex frowned but kept his tone calm. "Why not?"

"Because."

Alex shot a puzzled look at Taylor. Clearly he didn't understand, but he didn't want to say more and make the situation worse.

Taylor understood all too well and sighed. "Your husband threatened you, didn't he?"

"He said if I called the cops, he'd make bail and

come back and kill me." Donna raised her tear-stained cheeks to them and spoke around the ice pack. "And don't tell me to get a restraining order. I already have one."

"You might try going to a shelter. They can protect you better." Taylor reached into her purse, pulled out a card and tucked it into the woman's hand. She wanted to do more, but this was a step that Donna must take for herself. And Taylor knew all too well how hard it was to admit to yourself that you'd done everything you could—and failed. Somehow the batterers always made the victims feel guilty. If they could just behave correctly and do the right thing, the man wouldn't get angry, wouldn't hit them.

Taylor understood the psychology; refused to allow herself to be trapped in those feelings of helplessness again. She reminded herself she was here to do her job, not to rescue a woman from abuse—especially a woman who didn't want to be rescued.

"Was your husband home last night?" Taylor asked, curious as to whether Willard had an alibi for the time of the embassy arson.

"That's why he hit me. He came home reeking of smoke, and I asked where he'd been." She sniffed. "He assumed I was questioning his fidelity. Like I care. I'm happy when he isn't here. I was just trying to make conversation, but I should know better than to ask questions after he's had a hard day. And then when I told him someone else came by asking about him, he was furious that I gave out personal information." She blew her nose on a tissue. "I probably shouldn't be talking to you, either. If Mark finds out… Maybe you should…''

Alex picked up the questioning where Taylor had left off. ''Who came by asking questions?''

Donna shook her head. ''I don't know. He said he was from the embassy, too, and that he needed to talk with Mark about a special project.''

''Did he speak with an accent?'' Taylor asked.

''Yes.''

Taylor tried to keep the eagerness from her voice. ''What did he look like?''

''I just glimpsed him through the peephole. He had dark hair and was overweight.''

Taylor wished they had photographs of the general, the secretary of state and the security chief so that Donna could pick out the man she'd spoken to. However, even if the woman could identify the caller, the man's reason for coming here could have been legitimate. Mark Willard could have been working on a project with any of their suspects. And the security chief could have been checking on him out of curiosity, just as they were. ''Did your visitor wear a uniform?''

Donna shook her head. ''Please, you need to leave now. Okay?''

''Okay.'' Taylor stood, feeling obligated to ask one more question although she didn't expect a reply. ''Do you have any idea where we might find your husband?''

''After we fight, he goes to his slut's house.'' Donna surprised her with the direct answer. When she leaned over and wrote down the address with a shaking hand, Taylor wanted to hug her but she knew by Donna's squared shoulders that she didn't want pity or sympathy. "I wish he'd divorce me and marry her. Then he might leave me alone."

Taylor touched Donna's hand, reminding her of the card with the shelter address that she held like a lifeline. "There are good people ready to help you. But you have to let them know you want help."

"Please, just go. And if you find Mark—"

"We won't tell him we've spoken to you," Alex assured her, astutely guessing at her concern.

Behind them Donna shut and locked the door. Taylor squinted at the address in the failing light. "His mistress lives less than a mile from here. Convenient for him. We can walk there."

Alex looped his arm through hers. "A walk will do me good."

She heard the tightness in his tone, the outrage he was trying hard to control. Taylor knew he probably felt like punching the batterer. She'd like to give the man some of his own back herself. And the thought freed her—freed her from the fear that she would ever put up with abuse again.

She held on to Alex's arm, content to be walking at his side, feeling freer than she ever remembered feeling. Always, she'd avoided situations that had reminded her of her own past. She'd been hiding and there had been no need. She would never again be the helpless little girl that she'd once been. She'd known that intellectually, but now she knew it down to the marrow of her bones. She felt ready to face whatever the future held.

Her feet moved lightly over the sidewalk, her thoughts free to return to the case. "Just because Mark beats his wife and cheats on her, doesn't mean he set fire to the embassy. But she did say that he'd smelled like smoke."

"I know, but this is the first time that I've actually hoped someone that works for me is guilty."

Somewhere in the last thirty minutes, Alex had lost his laid-back attitude. Donna's battered face had disturbed him, yet he'd been gentle with the woman. And unlike most men, he hadn't insisted on telling Donna what to do. Alex had exhibited remarkable restraint in the face of his fury.

"I'm proud of you," she told him as they left the complex.

"I did nothing to help her." His tone was filled with bitterness.

"You didn't make light of her fears. You didn't assume you knew how to handle her problems better than she does. You were gentle and kind and you gave her respect. That means a lot."

"It's not enough."

"Sometimes that's all anyone can do." She stopped walking and took Alex into her arms. She sensed that he needed the contact. She wanted to give him comfort, and she felt that she could use some herself. Her embrace may have surprised him, but he recovered quickly, wrapping his arms around her and holding her close. Last week, a tight embrace would have felt smothering—but not anymore.

Tonight his warmth and solidity felt good, and she reminded herself that some men were decent. Alex was more than decent. He had a kind heart, one that was hurting for someone he barely knew.

Without thinking, she tilted her head up, and the comfort of their embrace altered. At first she'd sought to give solace. Now she wanted to assuage her curiosity and share the heat flooding through her.

He kissed her with a tenderness that made her feel as fragile as blown glass. Wanting more than tenderness, wanting his passion, she pulled him closer, deliberately deepening their kiss, letting her mouth explore, reveling as his breath turned ragged.

Her heart pounded against his—but not in fear. Her heart beat with newly awakened desire, with a feminine wanting and heat that made her give as good and as much as she got. She kissed him back fiercely, hungrily, like a starving woman who knew exactly what she wanted.

She wanted Alex.

ALEX PULLED BACK from their kiss, jammed his sunglasses onto his forehead, desperate to look into Taylor's eyes, needing to know she was just as overwhelmed as he. Their kiss had been electric, the arcing passion sizzling between them like an open current.

"Don't stop," she pleaded.

"We must."

With her face tipped up to his, he watched her eyelids flutter open. Her pupils were dilated; her expression needy. He'd never thought she could want him—not with such unfettered abandon. And he'd never seen anyone so beautiful that the vision scorched him.

Her cute little nose, her lips swollen from his kiss, and the wistful look of regret when he'd pulled back, had fired him into a blazing state of urgency that he'd never experienced.

She licked her bottom lip, and he almost lost his sense of reason. He almost forgot that they were standing on a public sidewalk. Her kiss, a kiss that held back nothing of herself, had him hot enough to think about dragging her into the bushes and tearing off their clothes.

Of course, he'd wanted her to come to him—but he hadn't expected this kind of passion. And he intended to be very careful with the precious gift of her trust. "Sweetheart, I want you." He considered rubbing his hips against her, wanting to show her exactly how ready he was to make love to her, but he didn't want to offend her tender sensibilities. "But this is not the place."

"Kiss me, again."

He groaned. "If I do, I may not be able to stop."

"I don't want you to stop."

"Can you hold that thought?"

"How long?" she asked, her voice melting over him like warm honey.

"Long enough to call a taxi and to find a hotel room."

She kissed his chin, his jaw, his throat. "We have to go find Mark Willard, don't we?"

"He can wait."

"No. When I make love to you," she told him boldly, "I want my full attention just on you."

He groaned again. Walking wasn't real comfortable right at the moment.

She tugged him down the sidewalk. "You know I never felt passion in my marriage. I felt trapped, pinned. *Wanting* to make love is a new experience for me. And I want us to make love. Soon."

She sounded so happy. She had no idea that each step forward had become quite painful. And that every sentence she spoke made him grow harder with need. "Can't we talk about this later?"

She ignored his request. "If that kiss was any indication, it's going to be good between us, don't you think?"

He couldn't think. His thoughts spun, and no matter how hard his heart pumped, he remained light-headed as every drop of blood seemed determined to go south. Alex figured he must be so out of control due to his recent spell of abstinence. Taylor's kiss couldn't be that special. One kiss had never before shot his testosterone to hell. But then he'd never kissed Taylor before.

Damn the woman could kiss. And kiss…

Gritting his teeth, unwilling to complain, he told himself he need merely think about—

"When we make love, can I be on top?" She giggled, mischievously and a little nervously.

—a cold shower. An icy cold shower.

"I've never…"

Her words must have elicited an unintentional growl or moan from him because she stopped walking and talking. From the streetlight shining on her face, he could see that her expression seemed uncertain.

However, he couldn't reassure her. He couldn't yet speak.

"Are you in pain?" she asked innocently.

He grunted, desperately seeking to regain control of the primitive part of his anatomy that defied rational thought. She must have taken his grunt for a yes.

She lifted her hand to his forehead. "You're warm. You aren't getting a fever, are you?"

She had no idea what she'd done to him.

"It's a hot night," he murmured.

"Would you like an aspirin?"

He chuckled, but it came out a soft groan. She began to dig into her purse. He placed his hand on hers. "Aspirin isn't going to cure me."

"It'll bring down your fever."

For God's sake, she'd been married. How could she not know what she'd done to him? If she just glanced at his crotch, she'd see the evidence of his desire, but no, she just kept looking into his eyes with concern and puzzlement. And if she was teasing, she hid it well.

She wrapped an arm around his waist as if fearing he would topple over. "Let's just sit down on the curb, and you can rest, okay?"

He forced himself to breathe in through his nose and out through his mouth. But all he could smell was the light scent of her shampoo, the clean mint of her breath and a feminine aroma that was all her own.

"Sitting isn't an option."

"Okay." She glanced at him again, then took out a tissue from her bag. Leaning forward, she mopped the sweat beading on his brow. At the same time her breasts brushed against his chest.

He moaned.

"You're ill."

"No."

She leaned into him and placed her hand back on his forehead. "You've got a temperature."

"That's because I'm hot."

She sighed. "You aren't making sense."

"I'm…hot…for you."

She took out her cell phone and called a taxi. "Mark will have to wait. Just hold on. We'll be inside an air-conditioned cab in a few minutes. Maybe you're dehydrated and the heat is getting to you."

"*You're* getting to me."

"You simply aren't used to—"

Taylor. Or the potent effect she had on him.

Interrupting their discussion, the cab arrived as if it had been waiting around the corner. Before she told the driver to take him to the hospital, he took her hand and placed it on his very hard erection.

She gasped, then chuckled in understanding and embarrassment.

"Where to, sir?"

Taylor didn't give him a chance to answer. Instead she boldly kept her hand in his lap. Apparently she wasn't that embarrassed. "Take us to the nearest hotel."

Chapter Ten

Alex had purchased condoms in the Hilton's gift shop while Taylor had checked them in. As she slid the plastic key card into the lock of their room, impatience swept over him. When the green glow by the knob signaled that the card had done its job, he opened the door, wedged his foot inside, then swept a laughing Taylor into his arms and carried her over the threshold. She flung her arms around his neck, her eyes full of promise, and then she tugged his head down for another kiss.

Reluctance seemed a mood of the past but he warned himself not to move too quickly. He vowed to watch her vigilantly for the first sign of hesitation or distress. The task he'd set himself wouldn't be an easy one. While he didn't want to cause her to withdraw or to change her mind, he ached to rip off her clothes and thrust into her.

He told himself he wouldn't lose control. He never lost control. Giving and receiving sexual pleasure had long ago become a well-practiced art. But he'd never been this eager, not even his first time, when the chauffeur's daughter had taught him about sex in the back seat of the royal car. He'd never felt this kind of desperation. Never had so much trouble kicking off his shoes.

Breathless, he somehow carried her to the bed. As she reached for the buttons of his shirt, he moved away and slipped the overalls straps from his shoulders. About to let them slide past his hips, he reconsidered. He didn't want to shock her with his lack of underwear, but then he realized that wouldn't be a problem, since they hadn't stopped long enough to turn on the lights. With the curtains closed, the only real light flickered from under the hallway door and the room remained dim, intimate and snug.

"Come kiss me some more," Taylor requested as she lay back on the bed.

"Yes, ma'am." Alex kept the condoms, lost the overalls, yanked back the covers and scooted toward her where she lay on top of the spread. For now, he'd keep the covers between them. Needed the covers between them to hold back. Her hands on him during the taxi ride had him ready to go, but he needed to make sure she was right there with him.

He kissed her, reminding himself that she probably hadn't made love in a very long time. Which meant that he shouldn't rush. He needed this to be good for her. But how could he think with her mouth urging him on, her hands eagerly exploring?

He broke their kiss, needing a moment to calm down. He tried to remember he had to go slowly.

Obviously impatient, she yanked her shirt over her head. Reached to unhook her bra.

He placed one hand over hers. "Let me."

"You're going too slowly," she complained.

"I'm not going near slowly enough," he chided her. "You've got a long way to go to catch up to me."

He found a tender spot on her neck, explored her pulse and the delicate ridge of her collarbone, barely easing down her bra straps in a sensuously slow, spiraling tease. She arched her back, silently demanding that he take more.

With his lips, he traced the lacy rim of her bra, felt her breath flutter and her pulse race. She threaded her fingers through his hair, striving to lead his mouth to the tips of her breasts. Through the soft material, he nipped her lightly.

"Oh, my." Her voice caressed him with silky hope.

"You like?"

"Yeah. I feel as if…"

He used his teeth again. "As if?"

"I want you to swallow me whole."

He nudged aside the lace, licked his way back to her sensitive peak. "We're going to savor this experience by going inch by inch."

"But—"

"I intend to linger right here for a long while." He blew on the tip, enjoying with his lips the feel of her nipple puckering even tighter.

She let out a soft moan. "Alex?"

At her question, not wanting to assume anything— no matter how needy she sounded—he pulled back. "You want me to stop?"

"You're teasing me," she complained. "It's not

fair. Now, that I finally want…want to have you…you aren't cooperating."

He grinned, ignored his throbbing sex and plucked at her other nipple. "I'm always willing to cooperate."

She clenched her fingers on his shoulders. "But I'm frustrated."

"Good."

"And I'm tense."

"Even better."

He finally removed her bra, and she let out a sigh that ended in a gasp. "This must be wrong."

That got his attention. He'd thought she'd gasped in pleasure and that he'd been doing just fine. "Why must something be wrong?"

"Because you feel too good."

"That's impossible." He bit back a chuckle.

She tried to tug his head up. "Are you laughing at me?"

"Waiting is going to be worth the ache. Worth gritting your teeth for. Worth tempering the heat in your veins. Worth holding back."

"How do you know?" She almost growled the words and sounded as sexy as hell.

This time he didn't hold back the chuckle. "Because I'm feeling what you're feeling."

"Duh." She clapped her forehead with her palm. "That's why you didn't need an aspirin."

"Now you're catching on. Surely, in the taxi, you knew I was aroused?"

"Yes, but I didn't know it felt so…so…odd. Good,

but odd. Light-headed. My muscles are taut, as if they could almost but not quite burst. And…''

''And?''

''I can't stop thinking about where you'll touch me next,'' she admitted.

Leave it to Taylor to try to describe her arousal. While she couldn't quite do so, he was enjoying her efforts, especially the little pauses and tiny moans that came from the back of her throat. Most especially the way she so obviously had to fight to hold still as he lingered and caressed. ''Can you trust me a little more?''

''Are you finally going to get kinky and take off my clothes?'' she teased.

''Actually, the thought's crossed my mind.''

''More than once?'' she asked, provocatively lifting her hips to shimmy out of her slacks. She hooked her thumbs into her panties.

He stopped her. ''Not yet.''

''Soon?''

He ignored the pleading in her tone. ''And for the record, I've thought about taking your clothes off *much* more often than just once.''

He trailed his fingers over the flat of her stomach and the hollow of her hips. She dug her fingertips into his shoulders, again. ''This isn't fair.''

''Are you complaining?''

''No. Yes. Maybe. How am I supposed to answer that?''

''Nothing like a woman who knows her own mind.'' He ran one finger under the elastic of her panties.

She trembled beneath his touch but she spoke with certainty. "I want a turn to explore you."

"Greedy girl." He let his fingers rove to her inner thighs. "You already had your turn in the taxi."

She parted her legs for him, but tensed. Alex had been watching for the tiniest sign of reluctance. He pulled back immediately, sensing she wasn't ready for more.

"What?" she asked him. "Did I do something wrong?"

He rolled onto his back, donned the condom, then laced his hands behind his head. "I'm not going to move again unless you tell me to."

"What?" She sat up and in the dim light he saw her scowl at him.

"I'm all yours," he told her, not daring to reach out to her. She had to come to him.

"Really?"

She might be confused, but she tentatively ran a finger down his chest, circled a nipple. He bit back a groan. He'd wanted to give her pleasure, and the freedom to go as far as she wanted. He ached for release, but even more, he yearned to give her a safety net, even though he was no longer sure if she required one.

He just hadn't expected lying still to be so difficult. He'd been aroused for almost an hour. And he wanted her so badly he quivered with the need for her and the release she could give him. But he held still. He didn't say a word. He barely dared breathe.

And then she continued to explore him with her fingertips, lightly, tentatively, curling her fingers in the dark hairs on his chest. Tugging softly at his nipples. And totally ignoring the part of him that strained for her attention.

He would let her do this her way—even if his blood simmered with desire, even if his mind clouded with lust, even if he died a little every moment that she made him wait. He couldn't ever remember wanting to hold back this much or the waiting being so difficult that he gulped air into lungs that didn't seem to work. He couldn't ever recall reacting so strongly to any woman, couldn't figure out what was so different about Taylor.

''You smell good,'' she told him, skimming her hands along his chest, dipping closer to his waist then trailing over his hips and down his thighs. ''And these muscles are from?''

''Riding.'' She stopped her caress. And he added, ''Riding horses.''

''Someday you'll have to take me for a ride,'' she told him, and from the throaty need in her tone, he had no doubt what kind of ride she wanted. ''But now I'm going to do the riding, yes?''

''Yes. You did tell me once that you wanted to be on top.''

''And you aren't going to move, are you?''

''Not unless you ask,'' he promised, praying he could stick to it.

She straddled his hips without touching the part of him that strained for her heat. He waited, not daring to so much as blink.

Still kneeling over him, she leaned forward until her lips remained just a centimeter from his. She whimpered softly, seductively, allowing her breasts to caress his chest. "You don't mind if I kiss you again?"

Mind? Why would he mind? Just because every atom in his body longed for him to clench her hips and drive into her? Just because it took every wisp of control he had left to hold still beneath her? "Kiss me, Taylor. For as long as you like," he added, feeling like a man who'd just given his woman unlimited spending on his credit card.

She didn't just kiss him, that would have been much too easy on his spiraling senses. She ran her fingers through his hair. She let him feel her hardened nipples against his chest. And she practically purred, rubbing against him like a cuddly cat.

Finally, when blood pounded in his head and his ears roared with the thrum of need, she lowered her hips and took him inside her. He'd expected her to take him in slowly. But no, she thrust down in one smooth move that almost undid him.

"Hold still," he begged. "You feel too good."

She ignored his request. "You told me that's impossible."

He had? He couldn't think. She was taking control of him, sweeping him away in a tide so strong he could barely keep breathing. Clearly she had no intention of stopping.

"Let me touch you," he half pleaded, half asked.

She grunted and he took that as a yes. Reaching between them he slid a finger between her legs, finding her slick and hot. She increased the pace. Despite his desire to hold back, his own hips matched her rhythm. He crested, rolling toward the inevitable, and then she found her own release, her muscles spasming around him, intensifying the pleasure, taking him over the edge.

When he could think again, he discovered that she'd simply collapsed on top of him. He'd curled an arm around her waist, and her cheek pressed against his neck. He waited for the urge to separate, but it never came.

Instead, he pulled the covers over them and fell into a deep sleep. When he wakened with her still in his arms, he had the urge to make love to her again. However, he suspected that after such a long period of sexual inactivity, she was most likely sore.

What surprised him most of all was that he was content to simply hold her as he drifted back to sleep.

TAYLOR AWAKENED WITHOUT one regret. Last night was the first time she'd ever relaxed enough to have an orgasm during sex with a man. Wonder and joy surged through her at her recollections of last night. Sex with Alex had been better than eating chocolate.

She supposed she could thank the playboy's vast experience with women from three or four continents. However, she couldn't have been more pleased that he'd known just what to do to reassure her.

But she refused to give him all the credit. She'd felt desire. And it had felt good. No, it had felt great.

She wanted to dance around the room and congratulate herself for this marvelous breakthrough. She'd actually had a good time. A really, really good time. Which to her meant that she'd recovered from a reluctance to date men, to kiss men, to touch and to be touched.

She hadn't been permanently damaged or scarred by her father's abandonment of the family or her brother's abuse or her husband's cheating. She was now free. And all thanks to Alex.

She would have kissed him, except that she recalled how much he enjoyed sleeping late and didn't want to wake him this early. Today was Saturday. No need to return to the embassy. So she let him sleep, eased out of the bed and headed for the shower.

After closing the bathroom door and turning on the light, she used the complimentary toothbrush, turned the shower on, adjusted the temperature of the water and stepped in. Humming under her breath, she rotated the shower head until it produced a steady rain. Ducking under the water, she almost wished she'd awakened Alex so he could join her.

Last night in the dark, she hadn't gotten a good look at his body, and she would have enjoyed marveling over it in daylight. While she soaped and rinsed, she realized that she couldn't have chosen a better man. To him, she was a woman with whom to enjoy a night or two of passion. He liked her, sure. But he would never feel more than that. She had to expect that a man who was notorious for his sexual exploits would end their time together without a look backward, without any hard feelings or guilt. He would move on.

And she would heal, thoroughly, totally, completely. She was definitely getting the better end of the deal. To her, Alex was an opportunity she couldn't pass up. She found him attractive and intelligent. She knew without a doubt that after he returned to his country and continued his playboy lifestyle, she would open herself up to the possibilities of dating, of finding the right man, and maybe someday having kids.

Meanwhile, she intended to take advantage of his prowess. After the last years of celibacy, she was entitled to a little fun. Knowing up front that Alex would never feel more for her than for any of his other women, that he would never commit to a woman, would force her to guard her heart.

MARK WILLARD'S mistress's home sat on top of a hill in an older section of Washington where the pace was slow and the streets shaded by huge oaks and elms. Houses perched on well-tended lots, the hedges high and imposing. Taylor had been expecting a seedy area, not this exclusive subdivision.

Instead of going back to the mall to pick up Taylor's car, they'd taken a cab. Taylor paid the driver, who'd stopped one block away from their final destination.

A roadblock of police cars, fire engines and ambulances prevented them from going closer. When a stranger edged up behind Alex, Taylor stepped between the two men. With her hand in her pocket, her fingers gripping her gun, she looked at the man's face, then relaxed.

Hunter! The ex CIA-agent had slipped through the crowd and found them, made eye contact with Taylor, nodded for her to follow him, then headed for the park. Beside her, Alex had seemingly missed the entire silent exchange. But when she tugged him away from the roadblock, he came with her willingly enough.

Bending close to her ear, he whispered, "How did Hunter find us?"

So he had noticed. Alex might be a laid-back playboy but he could be extremely observant.

She shrugged and kept walking. "I hope he's solved the entire case."

Alex kept an arm across her shoulder as they crossed the street. "Are you so anxious to leave me?"

"I'm anxious for you and your family to be out of danger."

Hunter led them through a path in the park. They passed one man walking his Boston terrier and a vendor selling ice cream, but apparently the majority of people had left the park to join the curiosity seekers staring through the police barrier behind them.

"What's up?" Taylor asked Hunter.

Hunter led them from the path into a more remote wooded area. "Mark Willard's mistress shot him."

"He's dead?" Taylor asked.

"He deserved shooting," Alex muttered with a hard look at Hunter.

"He's not dead. The police have taken her in for questioning, but the word is that she shot him in self-defense after he tried to strangle her with a garotte. The woman has two black eyes and bruises around her neck. Apparently she missed the region she'd targeted and shot him in the thigh."

Taylor watched Alex grimace despite his former

words that the man deserved what he'd gotten. Men didn't like to think about injuries in such a sensitive area. But she felt relief that Willard hadn't died. She still wanted to talk to him about the embassy fire and the garotte—which is what someone had tried to use on Alex. In her book, this was no coincidence. "And Willard had deep cuts in his side," she said. "Cuts that might match the broken lamp you used to free yourself from the garotte."

If she and Alex hadn't gotten distracted last night, she might have already completed the interview and the man in the hospital might be chained and under guard in his hospital bed. Now they'd have to wait until Willard came out of surgery to question him.

Still, they'd have another chance to question Willard and she couldn't regret last night. It had been too special. Alex had been a marvelous lover and she hadn't felt so energized in years. Her face must have revealed some of her emotions because Alex tugged her closer under his arm.

Hunter didn't say a word. Instead he took out color photographs of a silver sedan and handed them to Taylor.

She frowned. "That's the car that tailed us from the embassy."

"It belongs to Ira Hanuck," Hunter informed them.

Alex peered at the pictures, obviously trying to identify the driver. "Is Ira in that vehicle?"

"His aide was following you," Hunter said. "Possibly it's a normal security precaution. And it's also possible someone besides the security chief asked his aide to tail you."

"Where are Anton and General Vladimir?" Alex asked. Taylor realized that normally Alex would have known, but due to his downgrade in status from prince to handyman, he couldn't always keep up with everyone's schedules.

"Anton is currently at the Moldovan embassy, trying to work out details of a new agreement on how your countries will handle Russian refugees. Vladimir is planning meetings with his American counterparts."

Taylor handed back the pictures. "Any idea why Ira's aide was following us?"

Hunter shrugged. "I was hoping you could tell me."

Alex reached into his pocket and handed Hunter the disks. "We found these in the embassy trash."

"Moments before General Vladimir could grab them," Taylor added.

"Perhaps you can find something on them that we cannot," Alex commented.

"I'll try. There are several known terrorists in the area. We've been unable to determine who hired them or what their mission is."

"Great." Taylor sighed, unable to contain her sarcasm. "I feel so much better now, knowing that there are terrorists in the mix." She'd hoped Hunter would solve the case for them. Instead he'd complicated matters.

"It gets worse," Hunter warned her. "One of the terrorists is an assassination specialist. The scuttlebutt on him is that he accepts only high-profile targets.

We thought he'd retired, but we don't think he's here as a tourist.''

Taylor frowned. "He's in Washington?"

"Yes."

"Do you know who hired him?" Alex asked.

"Money was wired from Bulgaria to his private account in Switzerland. The Bulgarian government is very uncooperative when it comes to revealing information about these kinds of transactions. Our diplomatic corps is pressuring their government; however, realistically, I don't expect any help from that direction."

"Are we getting help from anyone?" Taylor asked, needing some good news.

"The Israeli Mossad is doing what they can. It's to their benefit to have stability in their part of the world. King Nicholas has also received a secret missive from the crown prince of Moldova."

"The Toad?" Alex asked, using Tashya's nickname for the man she detested.

The crown prince had wanted to marry Alex's sister, now Hunter's fiancée. No wonder Hunter's voice had turned deadly cold. Obviously he wanted nothing to do with the man who'd once thought of himself a rival for Tashya's affections.

"The crown prince claims that the newest treaty Anton Belosova has offered has insulted Moldovan leaders and could lead to war between the two countries."

Alex frowned. "That's old news."

"Yes, but the crown prince is claiming that the old guard from the former Soviet Union is funneling funds to the nobility that was once close to General Vladimir.''

Alex stiffened, alerting Taylor that he considered this problem more serious. ''You have proof?'' he asked.

Hunter shook his head. ''I'm afraid this is all rumor.''

Taylor leaned back on her heels. Hunter wouldn't have risked their cover or his own to speculate about rumors. While the news about the security chief's men following them in the car was troubling, as was the news of the terrorists, there was little they could do with the information. ''Do you have anything solid for us?''

Hunter reached into his pocket, withdrew a thick envelope, then handed it to Alex. ''Nicholas thought you might need some funds.''

''Thanks.'' Alex stuffed the envelope into his pocket without even looking at it.

Taylor should have been happy. Alex could pay her fee and reimburse her for her expenses. She'd make next month's rent. However, since she'd met Alex, her priorities had changed and her primary concern had turned from increasing her cash flow and bolstering her reputation to keeping Alex safe.

Although there hadn't been another attempt on his life since he'd turned himself into the embassy handyman, sooner or later his disguise would fail. For all she knew, someone had already recognized the prince and was simply waiting for an opportunity to catch him unaware.

Yet, if he refused to leave the embassy, she could

only stay close and hope for the best. Knowing that Hunter and his CIA friends were also keeping a close watch made her feel only a little better.

History had proven that anyone could get past the Secret Service to the most powerful man in the free world, the president of the United States—if the killer was willing to lose his life in the process. If Alex was shot and afterward she killed the shooter, it would be small consolation to her.

She wished she could convince him to go into hiding. Play it safe.

So his next words shot fear through her heart. He shook Hunter's hand. "Thanks for keeping us informed. It's time to get more aggressive."

Chapter Eleven

Taylor told herself not to fly off the handle. Obviously her priority and Alex's were different. She wanted to keep him safe and he wanted the identity of the man who'd tried to kill him. Reminding herself that Alex was her client and that she worked for him made no difference—not after they'd made love. She had never become involved with a client before; she had certainly never slept with one. She never thought she would behave so unprofessionally.

But now she had more at stake than just her professional reputation. Last night, Alex had been incredibly tender and sexy. She liked the man, was beginning to think of him as a friend. And she damn well didn't want him to get himself killed.

After Hunter left, they'd walked through the park to a busier street. While they stood on the corner sidewalk and waited for the cab she'd called, she took a good look at Alex. He seemed totally unaware of his stunning good looks. Even in overalls, he turned women's heads.

He would certainly leave her. That was what he did. What he'd always done. To think he might

change was a foolish dream that she would never allow herself. She'd already made that mistake with her
first husband, thinking that her love would make a
difference. Older and wiser, she knew better now.

Although Alex would soon be exiting her life, she
still worried about his future. She couldn't stop fret-
ting that he would attempt some kind of crazy heroics.
And to stop him, she needed to know his plans.

"You told Hunter that we needed to be more aggressive," she began. "What exactly did you have in
mind?"

"Now that the offices are mostly completed and
the primary suspects have moved in, we need to
search through their mail, their computer systems,
their files. In addition, I intend to search their private
residences."

"That's called breaking and entering. You can go
to jail for that."

"I have diplomatic immunity."

Great. She could go to jail. However, getting shot
concerned her a lot more than doing time.

"And I suppose you have their private addresses?"
she asked, hoping he didn't.

"Since I arranged for their housing, yes, I know
where they live."

The taxi pulled up to the curb and Alex gallantly
opened the door for her, seemingly blithely ignorant
of the churning in her gut. She could think of a better
way to spend the rest of her weekend, but she understood Alex's growing sense of urgency. The fire damage had been mostly cosmetic, not structural. With
crews paid to work practically around the clock, the

construction schedule would soon be back on track. Which meant that the embassy opening in just a few days and the visit of the king and queen of Vashmira must be made as safe as possible.

Alex gave the taxi driver an address. During the ride, he opened the envelope Hunter had given him. Apparently he hadn't just received a large sum of cash, but a small fortune. "Nicholas wired a bank, so we are no longer broke."

He might no longer be broke; however, her financial status remained unchanged. She refrained from saying so. She simply listened as Alex used her cell phone to buy a car. She'd never heard anyone buy a vehicle, sight unseen, over the phone before. The last time she'd bought a car, she checked out every used lot in town for the best buy. Then she'd dickered and haggled and had to arrange for a loan.

Money made the purchase as easy as ordering take-out pizza. She was amazed that Alex was so specific. He insisted that the gas tank be full and that the white sports car should be delivered to the same address he'd given the taxi driver. He'd arranged to borrow temporary dealer plates and insisted that the title be put in her name. He handed her the phone and she called her insurance company and added the car to her policy.

"Thanks." He squeezed her hand. "Don't forget to add the insurance to my bill."

She wouldn't forget. The premium for his little sports car was more than double what she paid for her sedan. She'd almost protested when he'd put the car in her name. But he couldn't very well use his real name and, besides, even if he had an international driver's license, he shouldn't allow his real name to be entered into any computer system.

Alex paid the taxi driver and they exited the vehicle. They were in a neighborhood that was a combination of old brownstone homes, modern town houses and luxury apartments. The new car he'd ordered was waiting for them. Alex opened the car door, flipped down the visor and caught the key. After trailing a hand over the sporty leather seat, he locked the car.

She tried to look unimpressed, but it wasn't easy. The car had to cost more than she'd earned in the last two years. "Whose house—"

"Condominium."

"Whose condo are we casing?"

"Ira Hanuck's. And we aren't casing it. We were sent by the embassy to repair the faulty electric wiring in his home office."

"Clever." She strolled beside him along the shaded sidewalk. "How do we know that Ira has a home office?"

"It makes sense."

Taylor restrained a scowl. Alex's idea might be clever but he hadn't thought it through. They had no idea what they were even looking for. When Alex rang the doorbell, she didn't know whether she hoped Ira was home or not. But if no one let them inside, then Alex would no doubt find some excuse to break the lock.

A short, stout woman with curly chestnut hair that had been fried by a cheap permanent opened the door, a feather duster in her hand. "What I can do for you?"

Alex showed her his embassy identification. "We were sent over to check the security chief's office wiring."

Taylor also had mixed emotions about going in through the front door. The security chief was bound to learn about their unofficial visit and, if the man was legitimate, he'd have them fired. If he wasn't on the up and up, then he would realize they weren't who they claimed, putting Alex in danger.

"He didn't tell me nothing 'bout it," the housekeeper said with a shake of her head.

"It must have slipped his mind." Alex attempted to reassure her. "Mr. Hanuck's been busy trying to find the arsonist who almost burned down the embassy." Alex leaned closer to the woman, as if by taking her into his confidence, he could convince her they were on the same side. "You can call and check our credentials if you like, but your boss is hoping there isn't a conspiracy."

The housekeeper's eyes opened wide. "Really? A conspiracy?"

"We want to make sure the people who started that fire didn't try to do the same thing here," Taylor added, holding back a grin at Alex's smooth flair for making up stories. He seemed to charm women naturally, whether they were European or American, young or old.

The housekeeper stepped back and opened the door wider. "Come in. Come in. Wipe your feet," the housekeeper told them, and Taylor realized that she hadn't overestimated Alex's charm. "Better yet, take off your shoes and leave them by the door. I just mopped, so watch your step." She led them through a foyer filled with furniture, new wallpaper and a hanging crystal chandelier that sparkled with light beaming in through immaculate windows.

Since the security chief had only recently arrived and the condo had a settled-in look, he must have leased the condo furnished. The housekeeper led them to an extra bedroom that had recently been turned into an office.

Cream drapes covered windows that faced the backyard. The room was painted a cream color with a dark gray border and had cream carpeting. Boxes of papers were neatly stacked in a corner. An empty file cabinet stood open. The desk, a massive, gray Formica-topped slab with black legs, didn't have a speck of dust on the surface. A new calendar that showed off antique guns hung on the wall.

Alex set right to work. He took a screwdriver from his pocket, unscrewed the cover plate from the light switch and revealed the electric wiring.

The housekeeper peered around him. "Is it okay?"

"This switch is fine. We'll have to check them all, as well as the light fixtures and the circuit box. We might be a while."

Taylor hoped not. The longer they stayed, the greater the chance that Ira would come home and catch them.

"Oh." Clearly, the housekeeper didn't want to leave them alone. "I've got a turkey in the oven that needs basting."

"Go check it," Taylor told her. "You needn't worry. The embassy people already vetted our credentials."

"I suppose it'll be all right, but Mr. Hanuck warned me not to let strangers inside."

"We aren't strangers," Taylor told her. She sniffed appreciatively, the aroma of roasting turkey reminding her of a time before her father had abandoned her mother and long before her brother had exhibited violent tendencies. Christmas dinner had been turkey. The delicious scent brought back memories of gifts under a tree decorated with homemade candies and topped with a silver star. Taylor, her little sister and her older brother had played quietly, listening to soft music while their parents set the table. Once, she'd been part of a real family, one she hadn't allowed herself to think about for years.

She reminded herself to call her sister, not to be too hard on her for thinking she was once again in love. She and her sister had reacted differently to their childhood experiences. Taylor had practically walled herself off from the male sex, while Diana seemed to believe that lust at first sight equaled true love. But that didn't mean Diana hadn't been hurt as badly by the family break-up as Taylor had been.

Alex waved a hand in front of her unseeing eyes. "Space to Taylor."

His action jerked her back to the present. "Sorry."

He held a stack of files, but gestured to the computer. "Why don't you see what you can find in there while I peruse these?" He didn't wait for her to agree, but opened the first folder and began reading.

She slid in front of the computer, booted it up, hoping the housekeeper wouldn't suddenly return. The computer blinked Password at her.

Alex peered over her shoulder. "Problems?"

She held out her hand. "Can I borrow your screwdriver?"

She turned off the computer and went to work on the casing. The entire time she wondered if the housekeeper would return before she finished. The case stuck, but finally opened with a scrape and a metallic thud.

Taylor held her breath but heard no sign of the housekeeper. She reached into the hardware and flipped a switch. Without putting the case back on, she again booted the computer. She waited, tapping her foot with impatience, hoping she'd bypassed the password.

Meanwhile, Alex kept turning the pages of a file. "This is interesting."

"What?"

"Our security chief has been watching the secretary of state, who's had several clandestine meetings with certain members of the Russian nobility—the same Russians who are funding Vashmira's Moldovan enemies."

"Wouldn't part of Anton Belosova's job be to negotiate with your enemies?"

"Yes. But he should have kept our cabinet informed of his actions."

Taylor detested politics. Politicians never said what they meant and rarely did what they said. Such scheming disgusted and confused her. She had enough trouble figuring out what she thought about issues when people spoke clearly and fairly represented both sides. A long time ago, she decided that she didn't like fanatics—any fanatics. But she supposed if one worked within a government, even middle-of-the-road people had to deal with the fringe elements, which didn't necessarily make Anton Belosova a traitor.

"Hmm." Taylor pulled up computer files. One with General Vladimir's name popped onto the screen and she opened it. But she couldn't read a word. "Help."

Alex leaned down. "It's Russian."

Taylor knew he couldn't read the hard copy files and the screen at the same time. "Okay. Since we're hooked up by cable to the Internet, I can run a translation program." She searched for the program she needed and marveled at modern technology as the words were translated into English.

She leaned forward with a frown. "It seems that the general also has contacts with your enemies. According to Ira's notes, Vladimir's made several undisclosed forays over the border in the past three months." She scrolled down. "Ira appears suspicious of Vladimir's intentions." She drummed her fingernails on the desk.

"What?"

"I don't know. Maybe this is way too big a stretch, but finding this information has almost been too easy. Do you think Ira could have planted this data with the intention of having us find it?"

"To cover his own actions?" Alex frowned. "I

think you're overreaching, although I suppose it's possible. I'm just not sure he's that clever.''

"Oh, come on. A security chief has to think at least three steps ahead of the other guys. And he sent out people to watch us.''

"Nicholas has been thinking of asking Ira to retire. He's not really up on the latest technology. Where you think breaking into his system was easy, he may think he's been smart.''

"Well, there are too many files here for me to translate and read them all. I could send them to Hunter but…''

"I'd rather you sent them to Nicholas. While we are friendly with your country, they needn't know all our secrets.''

"Do you really think the contents of this computer are safe?'' Taylor shook her head. "Since it's connected by cable, our CIA or FBI could extract any information they wanted, anytime they wanted.''

"I thought you had laws against—''

"We do. But they might obtain a search warrant because they're protecting a reigning monarch's life.''

The discussion ended as footsteps approached. Taylor barely got the casing back on before the housekeeper entered the office. The woman had brought them coffee and a plate of home-baked cookies. "Thought you might like a snack.''

She spoke to Alex, practically ignoring Taylor, which was all right with her as she tightened the last screws on the case from a position behind the desk.

Alex helped himself and bit into a cookie. "Thank you. These are delicious.''

Not even his compliment could deter the house-keeper from scowling at Taylor. "What are you do-ing?"

The sharp-eyed woman must have seen her fix the casing after all. Taylor stood and stretched. "The fire at the embassy started with two stripped wires from a radio. I wanted to make sure no one had done that to the wiring inside the computer."

Taylor had no idea if a fire could start in the man-ner she'd described, but if she didn't know, the house-keeper surely wouldn't know, either.

"And, is it okay?"

"Seems to be fine. But if you smell any smoke, it wouldn't hurt to throw the main breaker and call the fire department," Taylor added for good measure.

"Mr. Hanuck phoned to say he'll be home soon. How much longer will you be?"

"We're done here," Alex told her. "Thanks again for the cookies."

ALEX HAD DONE his best to charm the housekeeper, but he could still see a flare of suspicion in her eyes. So, he and Taylor quickly walked out of the security chief's leased condominium back toward the new car he'd just purchased.

"Do you think she called Ira and that's why he's coming home?" Taylor asked him.

"I'm not sure. There are several possibilities. If she called him, Ira will question us. I'd prefer to get out of here so he can't do it now and delay our investi-gation."

"If you want to search the general's and the secretary of state's residences, we can't afford to have Ira detain us," she agreed. "Of course, even if the housekeeper didn't phone him, she might mention our visit to him later."

"You may be right, but she might not say anything at all."

"Really?"

"I've often found that when employees think they may have made a mistake, they remain quiet to cover themselves."

Alex took the car keys from his pocket before they reached the vehicle. He wanted to avoid running into the security chief—at least until next week, when he might have some answers. Since the housekeeper had interrupted before Taylor could send Ira's files to Vashmira, they didn't have one lick of proof that Ira wasn't simply doing his job and investigating the conspiracy, just as they were. Alex was not pleased that the security chief hadn't discussed his suspicions about the general with the king—those unofficial visits across the border bothered him. Nor did he believe his brother knew of Anton Belosova's efforts to negotiate with Vashmira's enemies. For all Alex knew, all three powerful men had joined together in a conspiracy against his family.

When they reached the car, he started to place the key into the lock when Taylor grabbed his hand and pulled him back. "What's wrong?" he said, turning to her.

She peered at smudged fingerprints on the door of the shiny new car. "These might belong to a curious passer-by or a car thief who tried the door to see if it was locked, but—'' she frowned and bent lower ''—neither of them would have left smudges this low on the door.''

She reached into her purse and pulled out a compact.

Now was not the time for Taylor to freshen her makeup. He reminded her, ''We need to leave before Ira—''

''Wait.'' She opened the compact and angled it under the car.

Her action struck him like a hammer blow. Taylor wasn't putting on blush. She was searching under the car to see if anyone had tampered with it.

''Oh, God.'' She dropped the compact.

At the tension in her voice, his stomach clenched.

''Run,'' she gasped. ''It's a bomb.''

Curling his arm around her waist, he yanked her away from the car. The bomb could go off at any moment. Together they sprinted over the sidewalk and across the grass, racing toward the nearest cover, a huge oak tree in a neighboring yard.

They didn't make it.

The force of the explosion knocked them off their feet, but he never let go of her. They fell and rolled. He tried to protect her from the heat and flying debris by covering her with his body. He didn't quite succeed. Landing on his side, he curled around her, placing his back between her and the burning car, the flaming ruins.

For a few seconds he couldn't breathe. The blast had sucked all the oxygen from the air. His lungs hurt, his side ached and sparks landed on him like biting mosquitoes—annoying, but not dangerous.

Taylor tugged him closer, burying his head into her shoulder. Suddenly she was yelling at him like some crazy woman. He could see her lips moving, but couldn't make out the words and realized dully that the blast had damaged his hearing. She manhandled him, forcing him to roll in the grass, and she pounded on his back with her hands.

Slowly the ringing in his ears subsided, and he could hear her. She slipped off the straps of his overalls, yanked his shirt over his head, and then spun him around and ran her fingers over his back. "Are you burned?"

"I'm fine."

"You're sure?"

"I'm fine." The concern in her eyes made his stomach warm and settle. She'd been willing to risk burning her own hands to save him. But now instead of keeping her attention on him, she was staring at his charred shirt in the grass, as if he meant nothing at all to her. He was beginning to think he could spend the next fifty years with this woman and never understand her. Why wasn't she happily throwing herself into his arms and kissing him? They'd just escaped death. She'd saved his life with her quick thinking. He hadn't noticed the handprints and even if he had, he'd never have thought to search under the car for a bomb.

He yearned to take her into his arms and hold her. Hell, he needed to put his arms around her, to feel her warm flesh against him.

And she stood there scowling at his shirt. "Are you up to jogging a few miles?"

"Excuse me?" He ached to kiss her, and she wanted to exercise? He slipped the straps of his overalls back onto his bare shoulders, realizing that the blast and fall had stunned his thought processes.

She tugged him away from the blast. "Unless you're hurt, we need to get the hell out of here."

He'd forgotten that the security chief was on the way home. Automatically, he fell into step beside her. He glanced over his shoulder, confused. "Did you see Ira?"

"No." She jogged easily, her long legs setting a quick but comfortable pace. Obviously she didn't want them to appear as if they were fleeing the scene, but simply out for a Saturday late-afternoon jog. "Think. That bomb was another assassination attempt."

Damn! And then the conclusion she must have reached minutes ago while she'd stared at his burned shirt hit him like a lightning bolt. "Someone's seen through my disguise. How?"

When they rounded the corner, she picked up the pace. "When we ditched my car at the shopping center, someone could have lifted our prints. I assume yours are on file in Vashmira?"

"Yes." He thought hard, his intellect finally kicking into gear. "But I bought the new car in your name."

"With the weapons I'm authorized to carry, my prints are on file, too."

"Yeah, but how could they track us here?"

"Once they had my identity, they pulled up my credit report. The car dealer would have made a recent inquiry—even if you did wire cash. Whoever planted that bomb simply had to ask the dealer where the car would be delivered."

He'd almost gotten them killed because he'd wanted the convenience of a car instead of the hassle of taking cabs. "I'm sorry."

"It's not your fault. Sooner or later they would have found us, anyway." She glanced over at him. "How are you doing?"

He was tired. Damn tired and not about to admit it. "I was in the military. We didn't just sit around and drink tea, you know."

"Okay." She slowed their pace, tugged out her cell phone, then snapped it shut.

"What?"

"Calling a cab will give away our location."

"What do you want to do?"

"Steal a car."

She wanted to steal a car? There were some things the prince of Vashmira would not do. "No."

"We need transportation," she argued.

After all she'd done to help him, he wanted to contribute, and this time, he'd deal with the situation differently. "Let me handle this."

Chapter Twelve

Alex found and approached a neighborhood teenager out washing a Saturn that was used but in good condition. "How does it run?"

"Great." The teen didn't even look up, just kept washing the car, which obviously meant a lot to him.

"Mind if I ask what you paid for it?" Alex asked pleasantly as Taylor stood next to him, thinking that the last time he'd purchased a car, they'd almost been killed. But if Alex could negotiate a sale with this teen, and if he paid cash, there'd be no tracking them until she bought insurance and a tag and registered the title change with the department of motor vehicles.

The kid let off the pressure on the hose nozzle and plucked a chamois out of a back pocket. He began drying the roof in the center, working his way toward the edges. "I paid two thousand and Dad paid the rest."

"Will you take double what you both paid, in cash, right now?" Alex asked.

The teen stopped wiping the car and frowned at him. "I'd have to ask my dad."

"Okay." Alex didn't pressure the kid.

Ten minutes later they drove out of the neighborhood in a car without a license plate or registration. Taylor knew they'd eventually be stopped by the police, but a ticket was the least of her worries. To solve this case, they needed more information than they'd found at Ira's condo.

She phoned the hospital to check on Willard, pretending to be a family member. Upset, she told Alex what she'd just learned. "Willard reacted badly to the anesthesia. He's in ICU."

Alex turned right at the next major intersection as if he had a destination in mind. "ICU?"

"Intensive care is for the most critically ill patients. Willard may not make it." Taylor now realized that the delay in questioning Mark Willard might have been a crucial mistake. If he died, he couldn't tell them who'd hired him. And if he had been paid in cash, which was likely, they wouldn't find a paper trail to follow, either.

She'd been thinking so hard about the case, she hadn't even noticed where Alex was driving. Unfamiliar with this particular section of the city, she looked around for a landmark and saw that ethnic restaurants, boutiques and mom-and-pop shops lined a narrow street between condos and apartments. "Where are we?"

"I thought we'd pay the general a visit."

He'd driven here from the security chief's condo without taking one wrong turn. "Have you been here before?"

"I rented the house for him over the phone. And I've studied maps of your city."

Her eyes widened. Although there was much more to Alexander's intellect than he liked to reveal, his exceptional memory surprised her. "And you carry the map around in your head?"

He shrugged. Obviously he had other things on his mind as he changed the subject. "Without my tools, or even my screwdriver, it's going to be more difficult to be convincing."

Alex parked and they approached an apartment complex. "The general is subletting an apartment for the next two months. Unlike Anton, who is staying in a hotel, Vladimir likes the comforts of home away from home."

The dark street had only one streetlight. Tourists didn't frequent this section and the only activity came from the bars whose loud music filtered into the street. "In this neighborhood, your general is unlikely to bump into diplomats or politicians. He could meet anyone on the corner without fear of running into people he works with. I'm surprised you rented him a place in such a seedy neighborhood."

"The general has never cared for upscale accommodations. He wouldn't think of hiring a housekeeper like our security chief." Alex took her hand and peered at darkened windows on the north corner of a brick apartment complex. "He doesn't appear to be home."

Taylor pointed to a metal flight of stairs that ascended from six feet above the ground to the third floor. "We could try getting in through the fire escape."

"Good idea."

Even though the suggestion to use the fire escape had been hers, Taylor wasn't sure going up so high in the dark was a good idea, but kept her opinion to herself.

When they reached the stairs, Alex jumped up, grabbed them and tried to pull them lower. He hung on with all his weight. "They're stuck."

Relief flowed through her. "I guess we should go in the front."

"We can do this," Alex insisted. He released the stairs, bent over and cupped his hands as if expecting to boost her into a saddle.

Reluctantly, she placed one foot in his hands, and as she shoved with her other foot, which was still on the pavement, he boosted her into the air until her hands grasped the bottom step.

Alex kept lifting until she pulled herself up high enough to place her knee on the metal. After taking a deep breath, she stood and turned around to watch him.

"Hold on," he told her, then jumped. When his hands caught the bottom step, the stairs bounced. He swung his feet, bending at the waist like a trapeze artist then, hand over hand, raised himself onto the stairs.

His success gave her confidence to turn back toward the building. The first flight ended on a square platform where she changed direction and headed up again. By the time she reached the top story, her nerves felt as raw as her hands, which had been tightly gripping the handrails.

She told herself that the height didn't bother her. Her feet were exactly the same distance from her head, as normal. Everything was fine—even if she couldn't suddenly sprout wings and fly. She didn't fear falling—just splatting on the concrete sidewalk thirty feet below. Taylor took several deep breaths and refused to look down. Stopping at the third story, she tried to force her knees to stop shaking, then realized that the entire staircase was shaking from their upward progress.

Great. No doubt the city inspectors hadn't examined this fire escape in years. The bottom section hadn't worked at all, refusing to pull down, hopefully due to lack of use and not rust. She could only pray that the anchors pinning them to the building hadn't rusted through. She waited for Alex to join her and when he finally did, she had the sudden urge to fling herself into his arms.

Instead she steadied herself by clenching and unclenching her fingers around the railing. "Now what?"

Seemingly oblivious to the possibility of plunging three stories, Alex leaned over the railing to peer into a window. "We break in."

She'd been about to ask how, but Alex had already removed his shoe. Leaning outward, he smashed the glass. The breakage sounded loud to Taylor and the tinkling of the falling shards on the staircase served as another reminder of their height.

Alex broke out the entire pane, carefully brushing

the edges of the frame with the bottom of his shoe to remove any remaining shards. Finally he banged the shoe on the railing, clearing off the remaining vestiges of glass, then replaced it on his foot. "Ladies first?"

He wanted her to climb from the railing into the window. Of course he hadn't mentioned that a good two feet separated the stairs from the window. A mere twenty-four inches. The maneuver was a piece of cake.

Her mouth turned desert dry. "I could wait here for you."

He wrapped his arms around her. Her cheek rested against the heat of his bare chest. Against her ear, his heartbeat pumped to a steady rhythm. Gently, he used his hand to tip her chin upward and then his mouth swooped over hers.

She expected his kiss to be tender, persuasive, gentle. He kissed her like a thirsty man who couldn't wait another moment to soothe his parched throat. Taking, plunging, savaging, his fierce kiss got her blood pumping, her heart rate accelerating. For the next few moments she forgot she stood on a rusted staircase on the edge of a building where she was about to commit a crime.

She took everything he gave her and used his need to renew her determination. Right now, nothing mattered but Alex's arms around her, Alex's mouth on hers, Alex breathing life into her and infusing her with his own need to keep going.

Finally he broke away. "You okay?"

"Never better," she lied.

"Good. Take off your shirt."

"Huh?"

"I'll spread it over the sill to protect you from any stray shards."

With shaky fingers, she did as he asked. Still, she couldn't help but envision a helicopter's spotlight and a camera crew headlining her on the nightly news as she broke into an apartment wearing jeans and a bra. Telling herself the publicity would be wonderful for business did nothing to calm her nerves.

Once she actually focused on placing her hands on the sill, lifting her leg over the rail and ducking through the window, she felt more in control—that was, if she ignored the burning in her stomach due to her overactive imagination.

Now that she actually had both feet planted on the apartment carpeting, she worried over Alex. One slip and he could... He swung inside with the agility of an acrobat. She retrieved her shirt and slipped it on while he moved forward slowly in the dark.

The room, full of shadows from its furniture, smelled like lemon wax, fresh dust and burned coffee grounds. Alex flicked on a light, and she frowned and whispered, "Someone might see us."

"There's no point in breaking in if we can't find what we need," he pointed out so logically that she wanted to slap him. He didn't seem to realize that thieves required silence and darkness to do their dirty work. With the light on, she felt exposed and vulnerable.

But he had a point. She followed him through the bedroom into a long hallway and a den that the general had converted into an office. Alex began by pulling out the drawers of the desk. There was no computer, no file cabinets, so she checked the nearest closet.

She opened the doors and froze for a second. "We have a problem."

"What?" Alex kept digging through the drawers.

"The general has a silent alarm system." She pointed to the red blinking light. "When you broke the window, this system automatically called the police."

As she spoke she heard a loud siren coming their way. "You want to try and run for it out the window?"

"No."

"No?"

"You could be hurt."

Now he was concerned for her safety? "If we're caught here, we're going to jail."

Alex shrugged, as relaxed as if were conducting a state dinner. "You worry too much."

A bang on the door interrupted her four-letter curse. She strode to the door and unlocked it. "I'm opening the door and raising my hands over my head," she called to the cops. At least Alex had the sense to raise his hands, too.

Two officers with guns aimed at them entered the apartment. Taylor kept her hands high. "Officers, I'm a licensed private investigator and am carrying a weapon in my ankle holster." She made no move to retrieve the gun.

She knew these police officers were on edge. They had no idea if someone might jump out of the next room and start to fire a machine gun at them. They didn't know if Taylor and Alex were high on drugs, common thieves or about to start a fight. Trained to make hair-trigger decisions, the officers would likely assess the situation before shooting—but she couldn't be sure and gave them no reason to fire their weapons.

Alex kept his hands up. "What's the problem, officers?"

"Turn around slowly and put your hands behind your back," the taller officer ordered Alex.

"We aren't criminals," Alex protested. "My name is on the apartment lease."

The officer looked from the broken window back to Alex. He didn't lower his weapon. "Why didn't you call in the security code?"

"Because I leased this apartment for an employee."

"Right. You'll have your chance to tell the judge. Turn around, sir." The officer spun Alex and handcuffed his wrists behind his back.

Alex didn't resist but he kept talking. "Look, even if I were a criminal, I have diplomatic immunity."

"You have ID?"

"Not on me."

The cop rolled his eyes at the other one who had cuffed Taylor and retrieved her gun. "You have a license to carry a concealed weapon, ma'am?"

"Yes."

The officers escorted them to their black-and-white car. Alex didn't appear the least upset. On the other hand, Taylor was shaking. She didn't have diplomatic immunity. And if she was convicted of committing a crime, she'd lose her P.I. license and her livelihood.

"They didn't even read us our rights," Alex complained from beside her in the back seat, which smelled of sweat and old cigarettes.

"They haven't asked us any questions, so they don't need to Mirandize us," Taylor told him. "But anything you say can be used against you."

The two officers exchanged a long glance at her answer. Most citizens didn't know the particulars of the law. Right now, Taylor wished she knew more. Since this was Saturday night, she figured they'd be spending the weekend locked up. Bail wouldn't be set until Monday—at least that's what she thought. She'd never been arrested before.

On Saturday night, the station was jammed full of prostitutes, penny-ante drug dealers, runaway teens and a DUI. They waited to be processed while Alex got a look at the seedier side of the city. He seemed particularly fascinated by the hooker's accusation that the officer had taken her bribe then arrested her anyway.

Finally they were taken to separate desks where the officers filled out paperwork. Taylor sat close enough to hear Alex's entire conversation, which didn't go well from the start.

"Name?" the older partner asked Alex.

"Alexander, Crown Prince of Vashmira."

The jaded cop didn't bat an eye. "That's not what your ID says."

"My ID is fake. I'm surprised you cannot tell," Alex said conversationally. He was taking this as if it were an afternoon lark. Didn't he understand they were in trouble here? That he was dressed in overalls and sneakers, not an Armani suit. That they'd been caught in the general's apartment, after breaking a window.

"Your ID looks real enough to me." The cop wrote down his alias. "Address?"

"The royal palace, Vashmira."

The cop started to write, then scratched it out. "Your address in the States?"

"The Vashmiran embassy." The cop struggled with his patience, crushed a paper coffee cup and tossed it in the direction of his trash can. "Look, sir. I don't like filling out paperwork. I especially don't like filling it out twice. I'd appreciate the truth on the first go-round."

Alex kept his voice entirely conversational. "I don't think you'd know the truth if it bit you in the—"

"Alex!" Taylor warned him. "Can you produce the lease with your signature on it?"

"Of course."

The cop sighed. "Oh, really?"

"It's at the embassy."

She turned to the younger officer. "We get a phone call, right?"

"Later."

"Look, you all don't like paperwork. You might not have to fill any out. Let him call the Vashmiran attaché, who can bring a lease along with the prince's identification. Then you can release him, right?"

"Wrong. It's not my job to ascertain identity or to read leases. I just book thieves."

Great. Just great. The crown prince of Vashmira was going to jail on her watch. It was her job to protect him, and he was going to end up in a holding cell with addicts and drunks. If news got out, and it would, the tabloids would have a field day.

Meanwhile, he could be in danger from his cell mates. She'd heard too many stories of what happened in jail cells not to worry about his safety.

She'd had enough of this nonsense. "Are you officers aware that the Vashmiran crown prince disappeared from the embassy several days ago? That his guards were killed and that the prince's body wasn't found? Are you also aware that a Mr. Mark Willard was shot by his mistress yesterday afternoon? Willard tried to kill his mistress with a garotte."

"So?"

"Look at Alex's throat. That wound was caused by a garotte."

The two officers looked at the fading red line around his neck then exchanged another long glance with one another. Obvious, they didn't believe her, but maybe they were starting to have doubts.

Perhaps she could get past their cynicism. "And Mr. Willard works at the Vashmiran embassy."

"Nice try, ma'am. But that doesn't get you out of a break-and-enter."

Taylor shook her head. "You guys are making a mistake. The least you can do is put the prince in a private holding cell. If he gets through the weekend unharmed, then maybe you'll still have jobs come Monday morning.''

The cops didn't say anything. Their faces remained stoic. Alex leaned back in his chair, stretched his legs out in front of him and crossed his ankles. "How long would it take to pull up the prince of Vashmira's face on the Internet and check it against mine?"

Taylor couldn't believe that Alex's tone still held an edge of amusement. She really didn't want to spend even an hour in jail. The handcuffs on her wrists bothered her more than she wanted to admit. The thought of a jail cell door clanging closed behind her made her feel much too vulnerable.

For Alex, accustomed to every luxury, a jail cell would be not only humiliating, but offensive. Yet, to look at him, he seemed unaware of any discomfort.

The younger officer seemed to consider Alex's suggestion. His fingers moved clumsily over his keyboard, and then he squinted at his monitor. He stared at the screen, then at Alex. "Nice try, Your Majesty."

Amusement curled Alex's mouth. "That title belongs to my brother, the king of Vashmira. You may address me as Your Highness."

The officer chuckled, thinking Alex witty rather than truthful. "Did you know that the real prince has black hair?"

"I've decided blondes have more fun," Alex quipped, and Taylor couldn't quite keep the scowl from her face. She feared the police officers might suggest he could prove that he'd bleached only the hair on his head. But although the policemen clearly didn't believe Alex's statements, the officers treated them with a polite respect that did credit to police officers everywhere.

Which made her anger all the more difficult to suppress. These police were intelligent, so why couldn't they use their eyes? "Damn it. Look at his features. I know it's a computer image, but surely you must see the resemblance."

The older officer clicked his pen with impatience. "And I went to Vegas last week. You know how many Elvis impersonators I saw?"

Alex shrugged. "I suspect if one of them was the real thing, you wouldn't have believed him, either."

"You could simply check his fingerprints," Taylor suggested.

"We'll get those when we book you both." The young officer turned back to his forms. "Let's start again. Name?"

A half hour later Alex had given up his mother's ring and watch, and they'd both had their mug shots and fingerprints taken. On a busy Saturday night, no one would bother running them through AFIS, the national automated fingerprint identification system. It appeared they wouldn't be able to straighten out this mess until Monday when a judge set bail.

An hour later they were placed in a holding cell— a private holding cell—so maybe all their talking had done *some* good. Alex was confined to the men's side, and she to the women's. They couldn't see one another, but they could talk.

And the handcuffs were finally gone. Although there were no windows, the Plexiglas doors allowed in bright light from overhead florescents. Her cell contained a metal toilet bowl with no seat and no privacy from the male officer stationed to watch them both, a concrete bench and about ten feet of pacing room.

"Don't worry," Alex told her from his side of the cell.

"Why would I worry?" Just because she'd never been jailed before? Just because she could lose her private investigator's license? Just because she had no other way to make a living? Just because she was more concerned about his safety than any of the other stuff? Taylor stretched the kinks out of her arms. "At least no one can attack you while we're here."

"We'll be out within the hour."

"Your phone call must have been more productive than mine. Who's getting us out?"

"General Vladimir."

She'd thought nothing worse could have happened, but she suddenly sat down hard. "Tell me that I heard you wrong."

"General Vladimir has a copy of the lease," Alex explained. "He can also vouch for my identity."

"Have you forgotten the general is one of our prime suspects? That the man had a mistress who tried to kill your brother and an aide who tried to kill your sister?"

"Well, as you pointed out, he can't exactly kill us inside the police station."

The officer assigned to watch them ignored the entire conversation. He sat at a desk, going over paperwork. Taylor didn't know if anything short of a bomb blast would have interrupted his concentration.

"Okay. What happens after we leave here with General Vladimir?"

"What do you mean?"

Alex couldn't be this dense. He was deliberately setting himself up as bait. She realized that Alex wanted the general to make his move before the rest of his family arrived for the embassy opening in four days.

"You're hoping the general will try to kill you again, aren't you?"

"He's not going to succeed."

"Oh, really? Would you mind telling me why not?"

"Because we're going to outsmart him."

"We are?"

"Yes."

The prince sure could be cagey when it suited him. But she wasn't standing for his testosterone-induced state of we're-going-to-be-fine. "Just how are we going to outsmart the general?"

"I haven't figured that out yet."

A sudden sick feeling filled her with distress. Even the idea of him deliberately placing himself in danger made her physically ill.

She dropped her head into her hands. "Then we need to come up with a plan."

Chapter Thirteen

While they plotted, the officer continued to ignore them. A ringing phone on the officer's desk interrupted their conversation. The man's eyes darted to Alex, then he reached for the electronic switch that slid back the remote-controlled doors, which opened with a smooth swish—not a clang.

"Your Highness?" The policeman approached Alex.

Taylor rushed out of her open cell and watched Alex rise to his feet with the grace of a jungle cat. She would have thought he would be pleased by the recognition of his status, instead he nodded regally as if bored. "Yes?"

"Apparently we've made a terrible mistake. The king of Vashmira—"

"His brother," Taylor said with a jerk of her thumb at Alex simply because she enjoyed watching the officer squirm. It was mean of her, but she couldn't resist. After all, they had been treated like criminals.

"The king called our ambassador, who called our mayor who called the chief of police. The upshot is that you are free to go. Oh, you can pick up your personal items at the desk, and a General Vladimir is waiting out front to take you to the embassy.''

"We need our personal effects and my gun," Taylor told him. She required her cell phone to put their plan into action. She was to call the paparazzi while Alex took care of his part.

"Right this way." The officer really did look sheepish as he led them back down the corridor, especially when he held out a pad of paper and a pen. "Your Highness, may I have your autograph?"

Taylor choked back a giggle at the absurdity of their situation. Alex simply looked at the officer's name badge, then scribbled on the pad. "Perhaps you could be good enough to let me personally thank your chief of police?"

"I'm sure he'd appreciate it," the officer told him.

"And meanwhile, I'll go fetch our stuff," Taylor suggested. Alex's job was to delay, one he seemed extremely well suited for. Despite his shirtless state and the baggy overalls, when it suited him, he could play lord of the manor.

She signed for Alex's jewelry, his money and her purse. Thank goodness her cell phone batteries hadn't gone dead. Quickly she called several reporters and anonymously gave them the hot tip that the missing prince of Vashmira had been found by the Washington Police Department. She gave no other details, then checked her watch.

Alex not only had to stall to give the reporters enough time to arrive, he had promised to stay out of the General's sight. In addition, Alex had promised to set up a diversion that would prevent the general from immediately following them.

Taylor peeked around the corner of the busy hallway to see General Vladimir in his stiff, starched-and-braided uniform pacing impatiently. Deep frown lines between his eyebrows and beside his mouth revealed that he wasn't in the best of moods. Was he annoyed that his prince had broken into his apartment? Embittered that the prince obviously didn't trust him? The general could be an innocent man who had simply been called out of his latest mistress's warm bed.

He could also be a traitor and furious that his assassination attempt had gone awry. Right now, he could be scheming to betray Alex again.

She glanced upstairs at the chief's glass-windowed office. Wearing his watch and ring, Alex graciously shook hands and signed more autographs, and a few flashes told her he'd even posed for pictures with the officers. Good. She checked her watch. Twenty minutes had passed since she'd phoned the papers. Where were those sleazy tabloid reporters when a celebrity needed them?

She peeked around the hallway corner again. She wanted chaos, but saw only normal activity. General Vladimir continued to pace and to glare at anyone who approached him. A handsome black man with thick dreads and at least five carats of diamonds in his left ear, an alligator vest, baggy slacks and high-topped sneakers appeared to be bailing out an anorexic-looking woman in a revealing pink tank top and red leather capris. A drunk snored in a corner. One teary-eyed woman filed a missing persons report on her runaway teen. And several cops stood around a battered coffee machine, drinking out of paper cups and trading stories.

Finally, the exterior doors opened and several reporters swarmed into the room. There could be no mistaking their profession. Cameras hung from their necks and they held microphones as if they were extensions of their hands. Just then two women with large, half-exposed breasts latched onto the general.

Bingo! Alex had succeeded in hiring his distraction. Those two ladies were to remain by the general's side and call attention to him and themselves for the press. It had taken Taylor some time to convince Alex of the wisdom of the plan. He didn't want any bad publicity reflecting back on his country. However, she'd risk a little bad press to gain a measure of safety.

Leaving this police station would be dangerous. But less so now that the two women were flagrantly rubbing themselves against an astonished general who clearly couldn't decide whether to be pleased and flattered or frustrated and annoyed.

When the cameras began flashing, the general started shouting. Taylor glanced up to see Alex strolling down the stairs as if they'd rolled out the red carpet for him instead of having arrested him.

She waved to him, noticed that he now wore a police officer's shirt beneath his overalls and wondered how he'd talked the man in his undershirt into literally giving the prince the shirt off his back. He'd probably traded him an autograph, she thought sourly, then wondered why his adaptability bothered her, when she should be pleased since he'd made her job of protecting him easier.

However, she was anything but pleased. Male and female officers alike fawned over him. And like a spoiled cat lapping up the cream that was his due, Alex took the blind adoration in stride, accepting their smiles and handshakes and accolades with the grace of a…a prince. Damn it. She had no reason to be annoyed. But she couldn't help wondering whether he'd even notice if she slipped out the side door and left him alone.

She was jealous! And she didn't like what the green-eyed monster told her about herself. She'd grown more fond of Alex than she'd ever expected to.

But how could she not like the man? She'd bought him a hot dog for lunch and used clothing to wear, then turned a prince into a handyman. He'd almost been blown to bits, had stooped to breaking and entering and ended up in jail. Never once had he blamed her. Never once had he complained—treating the entire life-and-death episode as if he were caught in a fascinating game, all the while enjoying himself.

She resented those hangers-on at his side and didn't like herself for it. Didn't like that all she wanted to do was spirit him away to a hotel where she didn't have to share him with anyone—where he could kiss her and make love to her and give her all his attention.

The women Alex had hired were kissing the general, who now looked like a mouse caught in a cage. With the press out there watching the general's every move as they waited for Prince Alex to appear, the man couldn't very well shove the two women from his side.

Taylor backed away from the melee out front. Hopefully, Alex had so impressed the police chief that the man had instructed his officers to give them a ride. She joined Alex at the bottom of the stairs.

He reached out and grabbed her hand. Together, escorted by police, they hurried out the side door. She expected to ride in a police car. But there wasn't one vehicle on the street.

Her heart started to pound too rapidly. After the noise inside, it was too quiet. Too empty. Had they been set up?

OUT OF THE DARKNESS an ultralong limousine with Vashmiran flags flying from the vehicle's hood, flanked by a motorcycle brigade with their lights dimmed, quietly pulled up to the police station's back door. From Taylor's wary expression and her hand in her pocket gripping her gun, Alex knew she'd been expecting more trouble. However, he knew that only one man could be inside that vehicle. His brother, King Nicholas II, had arrived in the United States.

A rush of warm affection flashed over him. No matter the danger, Alex had known Nicholas would come. They'd always been close. Although Nicholas and Tashya would have been reassured by Hunter's message that Alex had survived the initial attack at the embassy, Nicholas would want to see Alex for himself.

Anticipating Taylor's surprise, Alex didn't wait for

the driver to open the door. He yanked on the vehicle's handle and gestured to Taylor. "Let's go."

He supposed he could have warned her, but as she slid onto the plush leather seat opposite the king and queen of Vashmira, he couldn't restrain a grin at the surprise in her eyes. However, she didn't relax. She didn't seem awed, but rather wound tight with worry.

Alex leaned forward and kissed his new sister-in-law on the cheek, then clasped hands with Nicholas. "About damn time you got here."

"Alex." Taylor elbowed him in the ribs. "That's no way to speak to your brother."

Well, no one could say royalty intimidated her. While Queen Ericka chuckled, Alex made introductions. But he could tell from the expression on Taylor's face that she was bursting to boss them all around.

"You people shouldn't be here," Taylor told them.

"Really?" Nicholas appeared startled for a moment while his wife lovingly tucked her arm into his. If Alex looked closely, he could see worry in her eyes.

Nicholas glanced at Alex, his expression darkening with questions at Taylor's forwardness. Alex simply shrugged. He leaned back, crossed his arms over his chest and looked forward to watching his brother deal with Taylor Welles.

She kept her voice even and polite. "You should both return to Vashmira and take Alex with you."

"Are you so anxious to be rid of my brother?" Nicholas asked gently, his keen blue eyes probing.

"I want him safe. I want all of you safe. You need

to delay the embassy's opening celebration until we figure out who is trying to kill you.''

Until *we* figure out? She'd implied that she wanted to send him home to hide and then keep working for Vashmira? He didn't think so. Alex rolled his eyes at the ceiling. For his effort, he received another elbow in the ribs.

Before Ericka had married his brother and become Vashmira's queen, she had been a political reporter. Now she often privately advised his brother on the best way to accomplish his goals.

At Taylor's suggestion that the royal family was in danger, the queen thoughtfully lifted her chin. ''So you think all the problems we've had are connected, too?''

''Yes. It's no coincidence that every member of the royal family has been targeted. At the embassy party, I assume you'll all be together? That Princess Tashya is also on her way?''

''She's with Hunter tonight, but she'll join us for the ceremony,'' Nicholas informed her.

''You're setting yourselves up as targets,'' Taylor insisted. ''I cannot believe Hunter is willing—''

''Actually, right now he's trying to talk Tashya out of attending—'' Nicholas said.

''If I know our sister, Hunter isn't talking right now at all,'' Alex commented with a soft, approving grin.

Taylor sighed and directed her frustrated comment to Nicholas. ''Doesn't Alex ever take anything seriously?''

Nicholas didn't answer her. His brother always had been a smart man. ''I thank you for your concern.''

He spoke warmly to Taylor. "In this troubled time, our family and country needs all of our friends' support. However, we cannot delay the ceremony to open our embassy. Invitations have been sent. Hundreds of people have made transportation arrangements and hotel reservations. Diplomats from five continents have already begun to arrive. It is vital that we prove to the world that Vashmira is a stable country. That people can vacation in Vashmira and trade with Vashmira without fear of a coup or of terrorism. Our allies will be there, and the royal family must attend to show we are not afraid of our enemies."

"You should be afraid," Taylor countered. "Not even the Secret Service can protect you from suicide terrorists. It's madness to place your entire family in one place."

"It's also an opportunity," Alex told her, knowing that her heart was in the right place. "If we know our enemy is coming, we can prepare to meet them."

Taylor shook her head. "I don't like it."

"I don't like it much, either," Queen Ericka admitted. "But Vashmira's survival may depend on strengthening our ties to the West. And we cannot do that without a viable embassy."

"But your entire family…" Taylor argued.

"I go where Nicholas goes. Tashya feels the same way about Hunter and, quite frankly, his help and connections behind the scenes may prove invaluable. And no one has ever talked Alexander out of anything he is determined to do. He and Nicholas are stubborn that way." Ericka softened her words with a slight smile, her love for her husband resonating with every word she spoke.

"I've noticed," Taylor rumbled.

Alex casually placed his arm around her shoulders and tugged her closer. Neither Nicholas nor Ericka looked especially surprised. But then he had a reputation with the ladies. They had no idea how much Taylor's friendship had come to mean to him.

He enjoyed the fact that she didn't need to look in a mirror ten times a day to reassure herself about her appearance. In fact, her appearance seemed to mean very little to her. She focused on more important things—such as keeping him alive when someone planted a bomb under his car, such as arguing with police officers to get him a private jail cell. She worried over his family's safety and stood up to his brother, apparently without a second thought. And she made love as if it were a fantastic dream. In retrospect, he wondered if the sex had really been that good. And decided they should repeat the experience soon.

Taylor nudged him and he realized he'd lost track of the conversation. "What?"

"We should keep your location secret until you must appear in public. That will limit your enemies' options."

"You want to hole up with me in a hotel for three days?" Alex grinned, cognizant that he'd deliberately put words into her mouth. "I can live with that."

To give Taylor credit, she didn't blush. In fact she squared her shoulders and shot him a look hot enough to melt polar ice. "It'll give us time to say a proper goodbye."

Nicholas grinned. Ericka sighed.

Alex restrained himself from squirming in his seat. Taylor confused him. He'd never understand the woman. The blaze in her eyes contrasted with the finality of her words. Goodbye? Who had said anything about goodbye?

"You can't monopolize all her time," Ericka insisted.

"Why not?" Taylor and Alex both asked at the same time, causing Nicholas to clear his throat to cover an outright laugh.

"Because she needs a dress for the ceremony."

"So, order her one." Alex sat back as if the matter were settled.

"She needs a designer dress."

"No, I don't."

Alex thought how good she would look in a custom-made gown. He recalled the overalls she'd picked out for him and realized it was his turn to get even. His spirits picked up at the prospect of Taylor dressing up. Buying a gown for Taylor was going to be so much fun—for him.

TAYLOR TOLD HERSELF that given enough time she would adjust to Alexander in his new persona. Although she approved of his close relationship with his brother and his obvious affection for his sister-in-law, the trappings of royalty made her uncomfortable.

After her father had abandoned her mother, Taylor's family had been mostly middle class. They never went hungry, but money had been tight, and extras, such as taking in a movie or buying a prom dress, had to be paid for by doing chores.

Taylor told herself that *things* didn't matter. That Prince Alexander was the same man she'd spent the last few days with, the same man who'd made such exquisite love to her. But her experience back at the police station had given her an inkling of what life among the rich and famous might be like.

The car stopped and she looked out the window to find that they had arrived at one of Washington's most exclusive hotels. Check-in wasn't necessary, and they slipped inside through a side entrance. A private elevator took them to the top floor. The king and queen had the penthouse, but Alex's suite stunned her. Huge bouquets of fresh flowers scented the living room, which boasted marble floors and floor-to-ceiling windows with a view of the city skyline. A glass bowl of fruit filled with ripe raspberries, ruby-red apples, dates and apricots sat on a cherrywood table that looked as if it belonged in a museum. In fact, all the furnishings—from the gilt-framed canvasses hung on gold-and-silver-threaded papered walls to the gold faucets in the guest bathroom to the jade carving on a white baby grand—looked classy and expensive.

"Why don't you take a shower?" Alex suggested, then picked up the phone. "I'll order up room service."

She wouldn't mind washing away the stench of her jail cell. A peek into the luxurious bathroom had her shedding her clothes without hesitation. A fifteen-foot-long mirror hung over a set of gold double sinks set in a marble countertop. She ignored the Jacuzzi tub, the steam bath and the sauna in favor of a shower large enough to house half a baseball team.

She helped herself to the basket of guest supplies and stepped into the shower. Not one, not two, but three spigots splashed water onto her, and the water immediately spouted out hot. The soap, scented with some exotic perfume she didn't recognize, smelled heavenly. A girl could get used to this.

"Knock, knock." Alex opened the shower door. "Can I join you?"

"There's room for two." She giggled. "Or three or four."

"Anyone else you want to invite?" Alex teased, his hungry gaze skimming over her soapy body with appreciation, causing her skin to heat.

She tipped her head back under the water, wishing she had a snappy answer. Just the sight of his broad shoulders, tapering to a narrow waist, and the long lean lines of his hips and legs had her thinking about making love. But it was the hot look in his eyes that had kindled her passion.

Alex wasn't just a fling. He wasn't just a man who had helped her overcome her past. Like a stupid twit, she'd fallen in love with Prince Alexander of Vashmira. Even thinking about his full title couldn't diminish the feelings welling up inside her.

Damn it. She'd allowed herself to fall for a man she could never have. Indeed, maybe the impossibility of them ever being together had made her feel safe. But now that she'd allowed herself to have those feelings for him, she was going to have to deal with them after he left.

She was going to miss him. Big time.

The fragrant scent of heather warned her that Alex had opened the shampoo, but when his hands threaded through her hair and massaged her scalp, she let out a soft sigh of pleasure. "I can give you an hour to stop that."

He soaped her hair, her neck, her back and her bottom. His hands grazed her thighs and calves, his fingers warm, knowing and oh, so clever. He knew exactly how much pressure to apply to cause an ache between her thighs.

She loved him. She loved the way he touched her. She loved the way he made her feel about herself, special and precious and coveted. And most of all, she loved loving him. Having opened herself up to caring about him, she'd conquered her past and banished her demons. Gloriously free, she spun around for him to wash her front.

This kind of happiness couldn't last. He was going to leave her. She'd known that going in, but she could no more resist his kisses or his lovemaking than the earth could resist orbiting the sun.

Had her fate been inevitable? Had luck brought them together just as destiny would tear them apart?

When his palms swirled over her breasts, when his thumbs teased her nipples, her thoughts shifted from the past and the future to this moment. Right here, right now, she could make love to the prince of her heart.

They had tonight, and she intended to make the

most of the time they had together. With her heart already full, she looked up at him. The heat in his gaze, the tenderness in his expression and the throbbing muscle at his jaw told her he wanted her.

And she loved him.

Loved him enough to keep her feelings to herself. Loved him enough to let him walk away without any feelings of guilt for leaving her behind. For a moment her eyes brimmed with tears that the shower washed away, but determined not to spoil one second of this special time, she leaned into him.

Gently she bit his earlobe, his neck, a nipple. She used her nails to lightly scrape his back and all the while she arched her back, allowing him free access to her breasts.

He smiled down at her. "I hope you are hungry. I ordered up—"

"I'm very hungry," she admitted. "For you."

"I'm all yours."

For the moment maybe. She quashed the thought. There were so many feelings she wanted to experience. She wanted to make love to Alex when they were both giggly happy, even tipsy. She wanted to make love to him when she felt ferocious and tender and sad. And most of all, she wanted to give him pleasure. Hot, unruly, wild pleasure that would make him lose control, that would make the blood leave his head, that would leave him in her power.

She reached between his legs, her fingers teasing up the length of his corded thighs, and cupped his heavy sex. He released a hiss of pure joy.

"Is that good?" she asked.

"Heavenly."

She lathered soap between her palms and ran her wet, slippery hands over his skin. Teasing him, seeing him quiver under her fingers gave her a heady feeling of power.

Alex groaned. He reached for her and she stepped away.

Then, she thoroughly rinsed the soap from his warm, hard flesh. And spun him around to face her again.

"I want you," she told him.

"Good."

"I'm going to taste you. All of you."

And she did.

Chapter Fourteen

The day of the Vashmiran embassy opening, Taylor had trouble keeping her thoughts focused as she made a precheck of the grounds and fingered the microphone/receiver Hunter had insisted she wear. These last few days holed up in the hotel with Alex, now, in retrospect, seemed more like a fantasy than real life. They'd made love repeatedly, refueling their energy with delicious meals and relaxing with long soaks in a whirlpool tub. And between bouts of lovemaking, Taylor had shopped for her gown—shopped without leaving the hotel. Exclusive boutiques had sent a van, a rack of choices all in her size, with accompanying accessories.

Alex had enjoyed watching her try them all on. And she'd enjoyed posing for him. Never before had she'd enjoyed feeling so feminine and had to tell herself repeatedly not to get accustomed to the royal treatment. While trying on the gowns had been fun, she hadn't the slightest idea what would be appropriate and allowed Alex to choose a deep emerald gown for her that offset her blond hair and gray eyes. While he'd been interested in the fit of her bodice, she'd checked to make sure the lower portion had enough fullness to allow her to strap a gun to her thigh without having it show. She was well pleased with the slit up the side that allowed her to take normal-size steps. When she'd checked the price tag and tried not to cringe, he'd told her not to worry. She'd assured him she wasn't worrying one bit. The cost of her dress would be showing up on his bill, as would the hair stylist and makeup artist he'd insisted on hiring.

Although Taylor knew security would be tight, she didn't trust the man in charge, Ira Hanuck. Too many difficulties had arisen under his watch and the fact that the security chief planned to retire after the ceremony just seemed too convenient. She would feel better after Hunter had taken over the job. Over a dinner with Hunter and Tashya, she'd learned how Hunter had impersonated Alex in Vashmira and kept Tashya safe. Knowing that Hunter was on their side made her feel better. The man oozed a confidence that had been gained through years of experience—experience Taylor didn't have.

Alex had told her that her job was simply to stay at his side, be his date, and report anything out of the ordinary to the security chief or Hunter. She intended to keep a keen eye on both the general and the secretary of state, as well as Alex.

Secret Service agents guarded the king and queen. Vashmiran soldiers in ceremonial dress uniforms and loaded rifles full of live rounds stood post at intervals along the perimeter of the embassy grounds. The high wall around the grounds formed a natural defensive barrier, but Taylor couldn't help wondering if the military men were loyal to both the king and their general. Those high walls could be just as much a prison as a safe enclosure.

The grounds behind the embassy looked lovely. A makeshift deck had been built and a white canopy pitched. A band had begun to set up equipment under strings of twinkling lights. An open bar stocked with Japanese saki, Russian vodka and even Chinese teas could serve the varied tastes of a multitude of international guests. From the gorgeous lilies and white roses in graceful urns to delicate finger foods offered by tuxedoed butlers on silver trays, the embassy staff had done themselves proud. Now, if the ceremony would just go smoothly.

Taylor checked her watch. Time to meet Alex, who would arrive with the king and queen. Alex had asked her to ride with them, but she'd wanted a good look around first. And as long as Alex was with Nicholas and Ericka and guarded by the Secret Service, she hadn't worried overly about his safety.

If anyone was going to make a move, she sensed it would be later, perhaps during the speeches, when there was a full crowd milling around to help camouflage a retreat. She patted her thigh, reassured herself that her weapon hadn't slipped, and headed for the front gate.

Alex exited the limousine first, and he immediately searched the crowd, his piercing blue eyes honing in on her. He looked so handsome in his dove-gray dress uniform and black leather boots that she swallowed hard. No wonder women adored him. And she was no different. She'd lost her heart, but she'd been damned sure not to let him know it.

Photographers had already gathered at the gates to await the diplomats' arrivals. Flashbulbs popped when she greeted Alex, but she knew that the publicity would focus on the new Vashmiran queen, who had returned to the United States for the first time since her marriage.

All eyes went to Nicholas and Ericka. Taylor took advantage of a moment of relative freedom to greet Alex. "Hi, gorgeous," she whispered in his ear when she really wanted to hug him. But a quick protocol briefing from Ericka back at the hotel had informed Taylor that the royal family didn't do much touching in public. A kiss, even one on the cheek, or handholding would be sure to end up in the tabloids. It would be hard enough to let go of Alex without being reminded of him every time she read a paper or tuned in to the news. Better to keep their relationship private.

"You look ravishing," Alex told her, then slipped his arm through hers.

"Any last-minute complications?" she asked, knowing Hunter remained in close contact with the king and that Nicholas would brief his brother.

Alex didn't get a chance to answer her as Anton Belosova joined them. The former fisherman who had become a brilliant secretary of state seemed to carry a heavy burden. The man always looked disheveled— even in his freshly pressed suit. The loss of his wife and her betrayal had aged the man well beyond his fifty-five years. Deep circles lined his eyes and the scowl lines between his nose and mouth ran deep.

"Good evening," Anton told them. "We are having good weather for a party. Yes?"

"Yes." Alex and Anton made small talk while Taylor continued to monitor the arrivals.

The king and queen welcomed their guests as car after car deposited people. While the English language predominated, she recognized French, Chinese, Arabic and a multitude of others she couldn't identify.

Taylor spotted the security chief wearing a suit and tie at the front gate, then saw him stride purposefully around the building. Meanwhile, the general held court with military men from several countries, and circulating servants attempted to usher the crowd into the building. With the night balmy, the breeze gentle and not a cloud in sight, Taylor wished she could have relaxed. Even more, she wished she could have followed the security chief on his errand, but she didn't dare leave Alex's side.

Princess Tashya, wearing a gorgeous floral gown, arrived a bit late, her eyes dancing with good humor as she hung on to Hunter's arm. Taylor had met the princess only once at dinner, but from their short conversation, she had no doubts they'd hit it off. However, it didn't matter. After the ceremony, the royal family would return to Vashmira. She wouldn't be going with them. Her job of protecting Alex, as well as their affair, would be over.

She would heal, she told herself fiercely. She would be fine. She would move on with her life.

Alex nudged her toward the embassy's front doors. "Shall we go in?"

"Let's walk around," she suggested.

He raised one adorable, aristocratic eyebrow. "Want to get me alone?"

"Something like that," she muttered, wondering how one man who had such an insufferably large ego could be so damn appealing.

Several other couples had the same idea, so any private conversation between them was curtailed. Taylor realized that a real group of gardeners must have trimmed the hedges, weeded the flower beds and mowed and edged the grass.

She and Alex walked together and with every step the strains of music grew in volume. Men and women danced on the back deck, but her gaze didn't linger on the happy couples.

She frowned as she peered through a hedge and spotted something white propped against the air conditioner condenser unit. "That wasn't here when I came by earlier."

"The air conditioner?"

"A propane tank." Taylor pried apart the hedge and peered at more gadgetry. She saw a blinking timer attached to the tank.

Oh, God.

She spoke to Hunter through her earpiece. "I've found a bomb. On the west wall. It's set to go off in five minutes."

"HUNTER SAYS TO get you out of here." Taylor grabbed Alex's arm, her fingers biting through the sleeve and into his flesh with urgency. She wanted to take him to safety and her tension communicated itself through her fingers.

Alex shook his head, his concern for his family and friends and guests skyrocketing above his own need for self-preservation. "We have to get everyone out of the embassy before it explodes. How far away will be safe?"

Taylor pressed her hand to her ear as she hurried him toward the dancing couples. "Hunter's people have found two more bombs." She scowled, clearly not pleased by the information she'd received.

"What?"

"They've already disarmed two and the third will be dismantled within a minute."

Alert security guards hurriedly escorted guests out of the embassy onto the back decks where the main festivities were being held. Oddly, no one appeared alarmed or panicked. In fact, people were drinking and laughing and talking as if unaware of the danger. The band kept playing and couples continued to dance. Clearly the security teams believed the danger was over, but had evacuated the building to be safe. Apparently, security had decided that informing the crowd and disrupting the party was unnecessary. So why didn't Taylor let up on her fierce grip of his arm?

Why was she urging him deeper into the crowd? Had she spotted a weapon? A stalker? And if so, why had she yet to alert Hunter?

"What's wrong?" he asked.

"It's just a hunch, but finding and disarming those bombs was too easy."

"What?"

"Those bombs may have just been a diversion. That's why they could so easily be disarmed."

A diversion? That meant she believed something else was about to happen. Sweat beaded on his forehead. Taylor didn't worry for no reason. He believed in her hunch, and yet he also understood her reluctance to say anything to Hunter without hard evidence of her suspicions.

She shouldered through the dancing couples, heading straight toward Tashya, Ericka and Nicholas. Surrounded by Secret Service agents, who tried to appear inconspicuous and who weren't succeeding, Nicholas shook hands with the Turkish ambassador.

Alex let her drag him forward since this was a direction in which he wanted to go. "Where are you taking me?"

"No one protects better than the Secret Service. Just don't stand too close to Nicholas. He's the most likely target." She spoke into the microphone to Hunter, "Why haven't you gotten the king the hell out of here?"

Taylor listened intently to someone speaking through her earpiece, shook her head, then looked up at Alex, her eyes pooling with anxiety. "The king has refused to leave."

"This *is* his party." Alex felt obligated to side with his brother, but that didn't mean his stomach hadn't knotted or that his hands hadn't chilled. He'd caught Taylor's anxiety and it rattled him.

"Why doesn't the king send his wife and sister to safety?" Taylor asked, winding through the crowd that stood more closely packed as they neared his family.

"You don't know Ericka. And Tashya is even

more stubborn. Quite simply, they won't leave unless Nicholas does.''

"Your entire family's impossible," Taylor muttered under her breath as they finally approached Nicholas.

Taylor's eyes suddenly went wide. She'd been looking at Alex, then spun around, peered into the trees and spoke through the microphone hidden in her ear to Hunter.

Alex leaned down to hear her say, "Oh, God. There's a sniper on a neighboring rooftop. The cream-colored two-story building with the green-slate roof."

She flung herself at Alex, wrapping her hands around him to shield him.

Unwilling to pry her arms from around his neck, he held her tight but turned them both so his back protected her. "Now what?"

"I saw a red light, the kind from a scope, right on your forehead."

Taylor was trying to protect him with her body. For a moment, pure rage that she would do such a thing rapiered through him, the emotion so primitive and savage that it rocked him back on his heels. A still rational part of his mind told him that it was her job to protect him. But this wasn't about a job. This was about his feelings. He couldn't lose her. Wouldn't let her put herself at risk for him.

Taylor tried to pull him over to the fence where they could take cover. Alex would have none of it. She'd told him herself that he probably wasn't the target. His brother was.

He yanked Taylor the other way, using his superior

strength to tug her along. "Come on. We have to tell Nicholas."

"He already knows." She tapped her ear, reminding him of the two-way communication device. Taylor tried to plant her feet and tug him back. "The Secret Service will protect the king. It's my job to protect you and I cannot do that if you expose yourself as a target. Can't you just for once—"

He kept tugging as she continued to protest and they'd reached his brother. One moment Nicholas appeared normal, the next, he wore the red light of a target on his forehead.

Alex didn't stop to think. He released Taylor's hand. Lunged between his brother and the sniper.

Alex never heard a shot fired. But all of a sudden people were screaming. And his legs felt like putty.

When he next opened his eyes, he realized he must have passed out. The crowds were back behind a cordon of police. He was lying on his back. Taylor was leaning over him, blood splattered on her pretty dress. Tears in her beautiful eyes streamed down her cheeks as she swore at him. Swore words he didn't know she knew.

At the blood on her dress, he winced and prayed the blood was his. "You okay?"

She smoothed back his hair. "I'm fine. Don't talk."

Cold chilled his flesh, his fingers and toes. So cold. "Nicholas?"

His brother knelt beside him and took his hand. "I'm here."

"The sniper?"

''Hunter's men got him.''

''Good.''

''Quit talking,'' Taylor ordered. ''Save your strength. The paramedics are on the way.''

She leaned over him, her eyes twin pools of fear. He tried to sit up to reassure her, but he was too weak. Tried to talk, but the words didn't come out. He needed…rest.

Blackness tunneled around his field of vision.

He fought to stay awake. Pain radiated through his chest and along his nerves. He told himself he'd been shot—not burned. It did no good as shock caused him to tremble. His head fell back as he gritted his teeth against the ice stealing over his bones.

Ice so cold, he flailed. Changed his field of vision. And spotted someone familiar in the crowd that stood silent and watching on the back lawn, a crowd being held back by a cordon of police officers.

How long had he been out? Minutes?

A man broke through to the front of the crowd. No one seemed to notice. Everyone was too busy staring at Alex, fascinated no doubt by his blood. Did they think it would come out blue?

He tried to grin at his own joke and choked on the blood in his throat.

Was Alex seeing things? Ira Hanuck appeared to be speaking to the crowd, but the roaring in Alex's ears prevented him from hearing. Beside the security chief, Anton Belosova appeared oblivious to the third man. A uniformed man with a gun, who stepped to the forefront of the crowd. No one else seemed to notice.

Alex tried to speak. Damned his weakness. His lips moved but no words came out. He had to… Had to…

Using his last remaining strength, Alex slipped his hand up Taylor's dress to her thigh, pulled out her weapon. Aimed. Fired.

The general dropped like a sack of flour, his weapon falling from his outstretched arm. And then everything turned dark.

TAYLOR HELD ALEX'S icy hand, unsure if he could hear her. "Hang on, Alex. Don't you dare die on me. I've never lost a client and I don't intend to lose one now. I'm not going to forgive you if you up and die on me." Her voice dropped to a whisper. "Please, Alex. Fight."

Paramedics gently shoved her aside. Someone threw a shawl over her shoulders. Barely realizing she was shivering, Taylor hugged it to her, her mind numb with fear. The bullet had lodged in Alex's chest and he'd lost a tremendous amount of blood. Hunter had packed his tie into the wound and applied pressure, but his face had been grim.

She hadn't dared to ask if Alex would live. The dark, shuttered look in the eyes of the men around her said more than she wanted to know. It had seemed to take hours for the paramedics to arrive, and when she glanced at her watch, she couldn't even hazard a guess at how much time had gone by.

She'd driven herself to the hospital, where she'd sat through the night in the lounge. Alone. Apparently the royal family waited elsewhere. She held no grudge. No one knew of her relationship with Alex or how deeply she felt about him. Information on the prince's condition hadn't been given to anyone but family members until 6:00 a.m. in the morning, when the palace press secretary announced that Alex had survived surgery and remained in intensive care, his condition critical. Alex wasn't expected to regain consciousness for hours, maybe not until tomorrow.

Knowing she wouldn't be allowed to see him, Taylor drove home in an exhausted daze. Automatically, she picked up the newspaper, unlocked her front door and collapsed on her sofa. The assassination attempt had made headlines, but she couldn't bring herself to read about it or to look at the horrible photographs of Alex lying on the ground.

She must have dozed. When she wakened, it was five o'clock in the evening and she flipped on the television news. Apparently General Vladimir had planned a military coup, but hadn't dared to begin his revolution while the royal family lived. Mark Willard, the man hired by the general to garrote Alex, had recovered and, hoping for a lighter prison sentence, he'd cooperated with the authorities. He'd tried to delay the embassy opening by starting the fire. His testimony and recorded conversations with the general revealed that Vladimir had assassinated King Zared I—Alex, Nicholas and Tashya's father. Then the military man had plotted to kill Nicholas and Ericka by encouraging his mistress to go after the new queen and king, and his aide to murder the princess.

A clean death from Alex's bullet had been too good for the general. Taylor viciously wished he'd had to go through the humiliation of a trial and been forced to spend his remaining years in a jail cell. History would label him a betrayer. A man reviled by his people. She hoped the traitor who had shot Alex would be buried in an unmarked grave and that his soul would be scorched in hell.

Fury and bitterness burned through her. She clenched her fingers so hard that she had to wipe tears from her cheeks with the backs of her hands. A video clip of Alex riding a magnificent stallion appeared on the screen. The television anchor's voice was solemn. "The prince has not regained consciousness. His condition is stable, but critical."

Stable but critical. What did that mean?

She changed channels but the news was the same on each one. Nervous energy made it impossible for her to sit still. She paced, tripped over a robe that had fallen from the back of the couch where she'd left it days ago. She picked up the robe and hung it in her closet. She tossed laundry into a basket and washed a load of clothes. She tidied the kitchen, scrubbing the countertops with savage energy. Then she swept, vacuumed and mopped the floors. Still, unable to rest, she tackled her windows.

Hours later, her hands wrinkled from scrubbing, her arms tired, she sat on the floor in front of her refrigerator, which she'd emptied and cleaned. She'd yet to put back the condiments when the news came on again.

She couldn't look at the clips of a healthy, handsome Alex again or it would disintegrate what was left of her already fragile heart. She held her breath as they recapped the news of the assassination attempt, waiting to hear about Alex's condition. "In other news, Prince Alex has regained consciousness. Doctors now say they expect him to make a full recovery."

Sitting on the kitchen floor between a bottle of pickles, ketchup, mustard and olives, Taylor burst into tears. He was going to live. He was going to make it. Relief so enormous that it stole away her strength seeped through her.

Alex was alive!

Chapter Fifteen

Taylor called the hospital the day after she'd learned that Alex would survive. They refused to put her call through to him, since he remained in intensive care. A kindly nurse told her only family members could visit, but people were putting bouquets of flowers on the Vashmiran embassy sidewalk and holding a candlelight vigil, if she cared to join them.

Numbly, Taylor hung up the phone. She wanted to be with him. She told herself Alex was drugged, hurting, not in his right mind. He couldn't exactly ask for her to join him at his bedside if he was unconscious.

She told herself to remain patient.

Three days later, she returned to the hospital, determined to sneak into ICU if necessary. She learned that Alex had been flown by air ambulance to Vashmira to begin his recovery. He was no longer in the country.

Although she knew that, in all likelihood, Alex hadn't made the decision to go without even saying goodbye, his leaving hurt. Hurt like a sharp scalpel that flayed at her newly won confidence. She'd always known he would leave her—but she'd never thought it would slice so deep or that it would take so long for her to stop bleeding.

The huge check she received from Vashmira and the thank-you note from King Nicholas almost seemed like a slap in the face. The only good thing to have come out of the entire incident was that the press had played up her role and her business had picked up—so much so that she'd hired a secretary and two full-time investigators to take on the cases she didn't have time to handle.

She tried to lose herself in work. Staying busy sometimes took her mind off Alex. But then she would find herself eating a hot dog or hear a reference to Vashmira on the news and she would think of him. And at night, she didn't want to sleep. At least during her waking hours she could repress her memories of Alex. But during sleep the memories flitted freely through her mind, making the days without him all the more barren.

Not knowing what had happened to him or how he fared drove her up the wall. She lost weight and couldn't sleep. She was afraid he remained unconscious or had fallen into a coma and that was why he hadn't contacted her. She didn't like even to consider that he was well and no longer wanted to speak to her.

In the past three weeks there had been no further news about his progress—just that he was recovering as well as could be expected. She wanted to phone Alex, but didn't know his location. Instead, she'd written a letter and sent it to the Vashmiran palace, but she had no way of knowing if he'd received her note or read it. As the weeks turned into a month and then two months, she expected the loss to ease. It didn't. She might not think about him quite so often, but that was because she'd trained herself to focus on the present.

Finally she received a phone call on her answering machine from Queen Ericka. She'd played the message repeatedly. ''Alex asked me to call and tell you that he is making a slow recovery. He will phone when he feels better. And I wanted to thank you for all you did for us...''

After two months Taylor had stopped leaping for the phone every time it rang, stopping racing to the door every time she heard a knock, stopped rushing toward her mailbox. It was over. Alex wasn't coming back.

ALEX SHIFTED UNEASILY in the back seat of the limousine. Perhaps he should have called. But there were some things a man had to do in person—such as thanking a woman for saving his life. Taylor had saved him several times, when she'd stopped him from driving a car that had been about to blow up, when she'd pushed him out of the way of the sniper's bullet and again after he'd been shot. Without her talking to him and demanding that he live, Alex might have just let go. Instead she'd urged him to fight for life and he had. The battle had been long and difficult, all the more so due to his location half a world away from Taylor.

He started to ask the driver to go around the block to give him time to gather his thoughts, but hell, if he didn't know what he wanted by now, he never would. He'd thought of little else during the long months of his recovery. He was here. It was time to let the past go and to think about a future.

He exited the limousine flanked by two body-guards. Since Ira had retired and Hunter had taken over security, Alex never went anywhere alone. However, as always, his guards were discreet and Alex understood their necessity.

The sight of Taylor's busy office took him aback. A secretary sat in front of a computer typing while she spoke through a headset on the phone. Other lines were blinking with callers placed on hold and the interior offices boasted the names of two new investigators' names in dark gold leaf on clouded glass doors.

The secretary looked up at him. "May I help..." She punched a button on her intercom. "Ms. Welles, there's a client here to see you."

"Did I forget an appointment?" Taylor's voice sounded just as Alex remembered, clear with just an undertone of huskiness and sexy as hell.

Alex was just about to say something when with a mischievous gleam in her eyes, the secretary shook her head slightly and raised one finger to her lips, signaling him to remain silent. "You're going to want to take this one."

"Fine, send the client on in."

Alex's bodyguard opened the door for him, looked around the office, then nodded for him to enter. Alex stepped inside and the guard closed the door behind him, giving him a smidgen of privacy.

Taylor sat behind her desk, her hair shoved back behind her ears as she frowned at some paperwork. She bit down lightly on a pencil eraser, her full lips pursed, her finely arched brows drawn together in concentration.

Alex didn't move. He didn't say a word. He just drank in the sight of her as if he were a man dying from thirst. The silky blue blouse and neat cream jacket suited her. And when she lifted her head and her gaze finally rested on him, her lower jaw dropped. Her eyes widened. She stared at him, the blood rushing from her face and leaving her skin a pale white.

He strode toward her, came around the desk, leaned forward and placed a kiss on her forehead. "Hi."

The emotions on her face changed from shock to happiness to anger in the space of a heartbeat. Blood surged back up her neck and into her cheeks, flushing her with high color. "Why the hell didn't you call me?"

"I'm glad you missed me, too."

"Alex!"

He heard the frustration in her voice and figured he'd better start talking fast before she threw him out. "Well, first I was unconscious. When I came to and asked for you, the doctors thought I was hallucinating due to all the medication I was on. Finally I asked Ericka to call you."

"She did." She stood and crossed her arms over her chest. "I'm not buying your explanation. But why didn't *you* call? You might have been injured, but you certainly appear to have recovered. Why didn't you call me last month? Last week? Yesterday?"

"I wanted to talk in person."

"You couldn't send me a note?"

"A note seemed…impersonal."

"You idiot. A note would have stopped me from worrying like crazy over—"

Her mouth was too luscious to resist. He leaned down and kissed her. Initially, his move might have been quick and decisive, but once he felt her lips under his, he took his time, savoring her taste, breathing in her feminine scent, lingering and wanting so much more.

As always, she responded to him, her hands going around his neck, her mouth softening, her tongue teasing and making his head spin. So when she dropped her hands to his shoulders and shoved him back, he was totally unprepared for her rejection.

"Stop it. You have no right to ignore me for—"

"Marry me."

"—while I didn't know if you'd lived—"

"Marry me."

"—or died—"

"Be my wife."

"—or knew how badly you were injured—"

"I'm very healthy and I can prove it."

"—and then you march in here and act like we've never been apart." She finally paused to take a breath and then she must have finally realized that he'd proposed. She fisted her hands on her hips but she'd gone pale again and her eyes had narrowed with suspicion. "Did you just ask me to marry you?"

"I did."

"We can't marry."

"Why not?"

"Because you're a prince."

"You're going to hold the circumstances of my birth against me?" He reached into his pocket and withdrew his mother's ring. "I hoped you would accept this as an engagement ring."

"That's a family heirloom."

"If you agree to be my wife, you'll be family."

She stared at the ring but didn't reach for it. His heart rose into his throat as she shook her head. "Thanks, but no thanks."

He felt as though he'd just taken a sucker punch to the gut. "You're refusing me?"

"Yes."

He wanted to shout at her, shake her, demand that she make an explanation, but then her eyes brimmed and tears rolled down her cheeks. Gently he took her into his arms and rocked her, smoothed back her hair. "I don't understand. I thought you loved me?"

"I do."

She clung to him for a moment then withdrew. She plucked a tissue off her desk and blew her nose.

"So what is the problem?"

"You haven't said the magic words."

Huh? Was she afraid of leaving her home and business? "Nicholas has made me the ambassador to the United States. We can live in your country for as long as we wish. I like it here."

"How nice. What else do you like?" she prodded him.

"I like hot dogs."

"Alex!"

"I like making love with you. I like eating hot dogs together. I like watching you sleep and waking up next to you in the morning."

Her face softened but then she squared her shoulders. "That's not good enough."

He held in a groan. "You want a title? Because once we marry, you'll be Princess Taylor."

She shook her head.

"Your own suite in the Vashmiran palace?"

She sighed. "We're going to live here, remember? And for a man who supposedly knows so much about women, you can be very obtuse."

"Ah, you want me to kneel and propose?" He kneeled, thinking he'd certainly made a mess of proposing, but if she wanted romance, he'd shower her with flowers and cards and...

She tugged him to his feet with an obstinate shake of her head.

Obviously he wasn't doing this right. "I could use a little help here. I can't read your mind."

"You haven't told me how you feel about me."

In frustration the words rushed from him. "You are the only woman I've ever asked to be my wife."

"So you love me?"

Damn! How could he have been so dense? A woman as special as Taylor needed to hear the words. She didn't want royal titles or palace suites. She wanted his love, and his heart lightened with understanding. He'd been afraid she'd ask for something he couldn't give. But his love? She had that. He might not be able to point out exactly the moment he'd fallen in love, but he loved her absolutely, unequivocally, forever.

"I love you, Taylor. And I always will." Her face lit with a wild happiness. "Now, will you marry me?"

"Of course." She kissed him lightly on the mouth. "There's only one more thing."

He arched an eyebrow, waiting, but his heart remained light as her eyes danced with happiness. "I want children."

"Agreed. And don't worry. I promise to love them, too."

HARLEQUIN®
INTRIGUE®

Elevates breathtaking romantic suspense to a whole new level!

When all else fails, the most highly trained, covert agents are called in to "recover" the mission. This elite group is known as

THE SPECIALISTS

Nothing is too dangerous for them...
except falling in love.

DEBRA WEBB

does it again with an explosive new trilogy for Harlequin Intrigue. You'll recognize some of the names from her popular COLBY AGENCY series, but hang on to your hats this time out. Because THE SPECIALISTS are more dangerous, more daring...and more deadly than any agents you've ever seen!

UNDERCOVER WIFE
January

HER HIDDEN TRUTH
February

GUARDIAN OF THE NIGHT
March

Look for them wherever Harlequin books are sold!

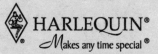

HARLEQUIN®
Makes any time special ®

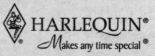

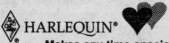

HARLEQUIN®
INTRIGUE®

Cupid has his bow loaded with double-barreled romantic suspense that will make your heart pound. So look for these **special Valentine selections** from Harlequin Intrigue to make your holiday breathless!

McQUEEN'S HEAT
BY HARPER ALLEN

SENTENCED TO WED
BY ADRIANNE LEE

CONFESSIONS OF THE HEART
BY AMANDA STEVENS

Available throughout January and February 2003 wherever Harlequin books are sold.

HARLEQUIN®
Makes any time special ®